Praise for *THE FINNO-UGRIAN VAMPIRE*

"A soufflé of a book."
George Szirtes, poet

"It is, among other things, a clever satire on the whole notion of Hungarian-ness, nationalism and the stereotypes of Eastern Europe, as Jerne, a hereditary vampire, is encouraged by her grandmother to join the family business...*The Finno-Ugrian Vampire* is played for laughs...many of them erudite."
Tibor Fischer, *The Guardian*

"*The Finno-Ugrian Vampire*, a linguistic tour-de-force and play on myths"
Rosie Goldsmith, BBC journalist and presenter of *Crossing Continents*

"...Szécsi's casual presentation of the completely absurd - in the form of Jerne treating most everything as entirely natural, even when it's not, works well given the odd premises of the book, and she uses both Jerne's vampire-nature and her literary one well...an odd, enjoyable literary-vampiric romp."
*The Complete Review*

'Despite having been published years before the whole Twilight phenomenon, *The Finno-Ugrian Vampire* could have been written as a tailor-made antidote to all that overwrought adolescent keening, with its refreshing injection of sardonic humour into the vampire vein. Vampy Grandma, with her silk evening dresses and painted toenails is a triumph, from her priceless anecdotes ('Me, into whose décolleté, Robespierre looked deeply, to whom Franz Liszt made an indecent proposal...') to the night when she chops up Grandpa, passing him through the electric meat-grinder at

maximum with 'the expression of a well-fed cobra on her face'. I also admired the novel for its linguistic inventiveness – its little flourishes of Latin, Italian and Hungarian – and its liberal use of literary references, from Peter Rabbit and Harry Potter to Kierkegaard and Oscar Wilde (a few Best Vampire Jokes are also thrown in).'
*Bookoxygen*

"...it pumps fresh blood into the anaemic arteries of the vampire myth"
*Hungarian Literature Online*

# The Finno-Ugrian Vampire

# The Finno-Ugrian Vampire

by Noémi Szécsi

translated by Peter Sherwood

**MARION BOYARS**
London · New York

Published in the United States and Canada in 2013 by
Marion Boyars Publishers
26 Parke Road
London
SW13 9NG

www.marionboyars.co.uk

First published in Great Britain in 2012 by Stork Press, London.

1 2 3 4 5 6 7 8 9 10
© Noémi Szécsi, 2002

Translated from the original Hungarian edition, *Finnugor vámpír,* by Peter
Sherwood

English translation © Peter Sherwood, 2012

Original paperback ISBN: 978-0-7145-3155-7
eBook ISBN: 978-0-7145-2330-9

Designed and typeset by Mark Stevens in 10.5 on 13 pt Adobe Caslon Pro

Printed and bound by CPI Group (UK) Ltd, Croydon, CR0 4YY

# translator's note

JUST AS ENGLISH is a member of the Germanic family of languages, so Hungarian is a Finno-Ugrian language, as are Finnish and Estonian and a number of the smaller tongues of European Russia and Siberia. The Finno-Ugrian languages are genetically unrelated to the other languages of Europe, as well as differing from them considerably in structure.

The name Jerne sounds something like 'YEAR-nay' but is not a standard Hungarian given name. Somi, a diminutive form of the male name Soma, is roughly 'SHOW-me'. Jermák would be the Hungarian spelling of the name of the sixteenth-century conqueror of Siberia, Yermak (or Ermac) Timofeyevich.

Peter Sherwood

# about the author

NOÉMI SZÉCSI is at the heart of the new generation of Hungarian authors. *The Finno-Ugrian Vampire* (2002) was her first novel, and a script based on the novel was shortlisted by the Sundance Scriptwriters' Workshop in Prague. Her second novel, *The Communist Monte Cristo* (2006), won the European Union Prize for Literature in 2009. *The Last Centaur*, her third novel, was published in 2009. Her latest novel is *The Restless* (2011). Recently Noémi has been awarded the state decoration 'József Attila díj' for her literary achievements, and *The Finno-Ugrian Vampire* was selected for European Literature Night 2012, held at the British Library.

## about the translator

PETER SHERWOOD taught at the University of London until 2008, when he was appointed the first László Birinyi, Sr., Distinguished Professor of Hungarian Language and Culture at the University of North Carolina in Chapel Hill, USA. Although primarily a linguist interested in the history of Hungarian and its closest linguistic kin, the endangered Siberian languages Mansi and Khanty, he has been translating Hungarian prose and verse into English since 1967. His recent translations include Miklós Vámos's bestselling *The Book of Fathers* and a book of essays, Trees, by the philosopher Béla Hamvas.

# The Finno-Ugrian Vampire, 1

## a were-tale

### for six actors, five voices, two players

*words to the reader by way of introduction*

AFTER THE DIFFICULTIES I have encountered in trying to bring my edifying and instructive animal tales to the public I would have sold my soul to get them published. Now I no longer have even a soul, as I passed on last spring, and I've been sucking men's blood ever since, just like my grandmother. I have, however, decided that if I were to write a story about my death, that might not perhaps prove uninteresting. Reader, do not doubt the truth of my words, for the tale I tell is a lie from beginning to end. It is often said that the only way to tell the truth is through telling lies. But in my view reality is wholly devoid of interest. Yet every word of this tale is true.

Respectfully: Jerne V. A.

# part I

## 1

I COULD call my grandmother cosmopolitan, since she has visited virtually every corner of the globe and everywhere felt immediately at home. But not every citizen of the world is likely to use a china tooth mug decorated with a map of Greater Hungary and the irredentist slogan 'Transylvania is Ours!' Because that's what my Grandmother is like. She comes home at dawn having gorged herself, and uses this mug to rinse out her mouth. Sometimes she wakes me up with the noise of her gargling.

And that's just how it was that morning. I stumbled out to the bathroom as I was, in my nightgown. It was a quarter past five. Grandma was just stripping away the layers of make-up she had plastered over her intense beauty. Because she is gorgeous, like a newly-restored porcelain doll. As the slinky little silk evening dress slid from her slim body, Grandma glittered in all her unvarnished glory and I just stood there awkwardly in the cotton nightdress that I wore now that the autumn nights were drawing in but before the district's central heating had been switched on.

'You're late, Gran,' I said pointedly.

'Yes, I'm absolutely livid. This fellow tonight was an absolute disaster. I tried every trick in the book, body language and all, before he realized where I was headed. To cap it all, he lived out in the back of beyond and once I was done I had to wait an hour for a taxi. Meanwhile I watched him bleed dry. Once he'd snuffed it, I left.'

'Please, spare me the details.'

Sometimes when I think of blood, I feel quite ill. Nauseated. In my mind's eye I can see the gaping wounds, and it's as if it was me the blood was draining out of. It makes me grow faint.

'No good turning your nose up. You'll get to like the taste sooner or later.'

'I hope so, Gran.'

It may sound odd for someone like me to address this *femme fatale* impertinently as Grandmother. However, for one thing it is a fact that we were family and for another Grandma already had more than thirty-three names, none of which she was particularly attached to, while her grandmotherhood was permanent, like the stars in the sky. And for another thing, I always got confused about whether at any particular time she was being Lilith, Lamia or Empusa.

'Look at me. Don't I look terrific?' Grandma forced me to look her in the face. Her lips were still damp and swollen. 'That's from the regular consumption of fresh blood. It's packed with iron and minerals. And now just take a look at yourself,' she went on. 'Your hair is falling out and tired, you're thin as a rake, and that makes your nose stick out of your face even more.'

I turned my head away, repelled by the sight of the bloody mouth. Grandma caught my glance and looked deep into my eyes.

'You must suck out their blood before they suck out yours.'

That was scary. I went off to make some hot chocolate, wondering who I was to consider as the general subject of that sentence as I measured out the chocolate and the sugar. That's the kind of thing I drink, as I am still alive. Grandma has been among the living dead for at least two hundred years, so everything she eats tastes like sawdust to her, except for human blood, of course, which is truly flavorsome.

I sat down on my bed, mug in hand. From the window of my small attic room I could see the bare trees bathed by the light of the rising sun. For this nation the City Park in Pest commemorates the most glorious days of its history. Here, in 1896, the Hungarians celebrated what some scholars said was the thousand-year anniversary of the arrival of their ancestors in their present-day homeland (the exact month and day they've still not managed to work out).

And then they *fecerunt magnum áldomás*, had a huge blow-out, as some chronicle or other said. Or was that not in 896? I was always bad at Hungarian history but as a child I was very much taken with the story of the seven Magyar chieftains commingling their blood in a goblet and drinking to seal their alliance. During my years in the wilderness, when I was trying to find myself, it was ample justification to me that my family's activities in this country were not without precedent. Pretty much nothing can happen without tradition of some kind.

But in this country there is always something to celebrate. The climate is excellent. It's cold in winter and hot in summer. In the autumn it rains and in the spring the weather is unpredictable. This is something I've considered carefully: in my opinion the only thing it lacks is the sea, which would boost the economy through tourism, make for cheaper squid, and enable Hungarian yachtsmen to reach the top rankings in international competitions. On the other hand, it would be annoying if the fig trees were to blossom like mad, twice a year.

Although these Finno-Ugrian people did not fight back with appropriate militancy when they were pincered by aggressive Slavonic and Germanic hordes, Hungary now occupies one of the prime locations in the region. It has wheat with a high gluten content, fructose-rich fruit, wild steeds roam its plains, and fat Hungarian hogs and cattle feed on the mirage-haunted *Puszta*. Actually, I have yet to see that *Fata Morgana* but I'm not bothered. Anyhow, the climate is very good for agriculture; this is a rich land.

Grandma had lived in the area around City Park before, at the time of the millennial celebrations, and a number of her unforgettable blood-sucking memories were closely bound up with the Old Buda Castle nightclub. So when she returned to Hungary on the occasion of one of the country's National Deaths – I can't now remember which – she was unwilling to lodge anywhere but her old haunts around the park. As for the choice of city, she didn't hesitate for a moment: in this country there's no point living anywhere but the capital, Budapest. I really don't understand what the other eight million Hungarians are doing down there in the countryside. I've never been beyond Budapest's city limits, or at least not further than the airport, but to my mind those country folks must surely all be wallowing around in the mud and dreaming of one day moving up to the Hungarian metropolis.

So, giving the lie to those vaunted vampire legends, we don't live in some ruined castle. These days even vampires try to find sensible solutions and who wants to spend a fortune on gas, water and electricity? The house where we have a top floor apartment has every modern convenience and is in excellent condition, thanks to the house representative's contacts and string-pulling. The plaster is not peeling off, the walls are not covered in saltpetre and the balconies don't need shoring up from the outside.

Nevertheless, a large colony of rats can often be encountered in the stairwell. No wonder: Grandma feeds them, as their presence is vital to her image. In practice they would consume anything, but Grandma tends to spoil them with special treats that she reserves for her household pets. We also made an effort to soften the air of sterility exuded by the excessive care that has been lavished on the building. One summer we knocked the plaster off the part of the stairwell leading to our apartment and doused the walls with ditchwater until they gave off a suitably penetrating smell of mould. Grandma even insisted on gouging a few bullet holes in the cement. Admittedly, we could have chosen a building already possessed of these attributes, but most of those currently provide homes for the proletariat, and at least we had the added bonus of enjoying our own handiwork.

# 2

DAY WAS BREAKING. It was not a particularly significant day one way or the other, but if I have after all to designate a point, a nail sticking out of the wall, on which I can hang the thread of my tale, this would seem to be as good as any. It was from here that I set out to acquire knowledge and to experience the world, which is the perverse desire of every humanoid possessed of natural instincts.

I swished the hot chocolate round in my cup for a while, finished it off with a decisive gulp, and went back to Grandma. She had already settled into her coffin but had not yet drawn the lid over it. She launched into her usual gripe.

'I've got to get up early again, before the stock exchange closes. In the old days I could pass myself off as a widow and live without a care. Like a merry widow.' Then she began to croon a snatch from a different operetta: '*Wiener Blut, Wiener Blut...* No one asked where my money came from and I could go wherever I pleased. Now? I have to live at night and work during the day.'

'Don't go on so! You've plenty to keep you going.'

'That's true,' she conceded, and tried to find a more comfortable position in the coffin. 'Still, sometimes I feel I just can't keep up. I hate this damned women's lib business.'

'It's no love-fest, that's for sure.'

'It's all right for me, I don't get old, but it will be the death of these mortal women.'

'Or not, as the case may be.'

'Oh, well. Let's call it a day. Get on with your work, Jerne!' she said and closed the coffin lid.

I set about my morning chores and soon set off for work. I have no choice but to work, just like poor Grandma, even though we are rolling in money. For vampires need some kind of job as a cover. This ensures that officialdom is suitably deceived and also offers an opportunity for social intercourse, vital for the purposes of identifying and securing future victims.

Grandma plays the stock exchange with a modest sum, just for form's sake. This is not too much of a problem for her, as she has always operated in the financial and economic sector, sometimes as a rich heiress, sometimes as a rich widow. She is good with money. But when it was time for me to choose a career, that is, when it was time to select my own cover activity, my grandparent and guardian thought that the entrepreneurial sphere and the world of finance were not for my sensitive soul. If I had to do something, it would have to be, rather, in the world of the arts.

The stage was dismissed at once, as it would have put me too much into the limelight and my vampirism would have attracted immediate attention. And however great my enthusiasm for the world of painting – indeed, I dabbled myself, limning charming crowd scenes – it turned out that my sense of form and color did not mark me out for any branch of either the fine or the applied arts. It also became crystal clear that neither my pointed and sizeable auricular appendages nor my sheer love of song were any substitute for an ear for music. In the end the choice fell on an area that many see as situated at the intersection of the arts and the sciences: specifically, the world of literature. This was an excellent decision, especially when one does not actually have to earn one's living from it. And that's not intended to be subtly ironic: I really don't want to have to work for a living. I want to work just so that it will look as though I'm making a living from my labors. And that's why I must devote myself to an extraordinarily wide range of extraordinarily time-consuming matters.

Difficult, but not impossible, since everyone can write. Even me. Especially stories, because stories are straightforward and their language is simple. I'm careful though not to write anything too good, as I don't want to draw attention to myself under any circumstances. I write just so that if anyone should ask 'And what do you do for a living?' I can reply:

'I write stories about Initiative, the bumptious but cowardly rabbit.'

'And you can make a living from that?' comes the usual response, as this is what Hungarians are especially interested in.

'No,' I reply, to reassure them, as I know how distressing it can be if someone is doing well (particularly an idle scribbler!) and then I add:

'And I work in a publishing house.'

That is indeed the case. It was my second day at the publisher Elektra and Co. I was the sole employee at a firm with a management consisting of two people: Elektra and her Co. I had obtained this position by posting an advertisement as follows:

*Recent graduate, inexperienced beginner, seeks modestly paid employment offering no challenges or responsibilities.*

I had two replies and for a short while I was gripped by decidophobia, unable to choose between translating romantic novels and correcting spelling mistakes in horoscopes. In the end I realized that, of the two, I found esoterica the less repellent. In the case of romances what I found distressing was not so much that they are read only by women, but that these are the books containing the sentences that most rapidly make me want to vomit. I feared that if I spent too much time in close proximity to such texts, I too would start saying things like 'I like you because you make me laugh' and 'You made me cry. You broke my heart.' And to cap it all, these novels are indeed blood-chillingly accurate in their representation of reality: people really do regale each other with such drivel when that mysterious chemistry gets going.

I didn't want work that made use of my brains, as I wanted to save my intellectual energy for the world of stories. It was a bonus that the publishing house, which specialized chiefly in popular psychology and the occult, was within walking distance of where I lived and it cheered me up to think how invigorating it would be to start each day with a brisk little walk.

'My partner.' That was how Norma-Elektra, the editor-in-chief, referred to her co-owner with a demure smile. I had not yet met the person in question. In the office it seemed that it was Norma-Elektra who held the fort. She was one of those women who, if you meet them three times, despite spending hours talking to them, the fourth time you will pass them in the street without noticing. I know, because that's what happened to me that morning. And that's also how I discovered she could give you a really piercing stare. This is as much as I want to say about her by way of introduction at this point.

Norma-Elektra was just off to secure the rights to a self-help book at the top of the *New York Times* bestseller list when a moderately repulsive and quite strapping figure of a man entered the three-room apartment that was home to the enterprise. They gave each other a neutral, domestic peck on the cheek, the woman left, and the man turned towards me.

'So, you are Jerne. That is your name isn't it? I'm Jermák.'

I disapprove of such immediate intimacy on a first encounter; still, I did introduce myself.

'Well, and how do you like the work?'

'It's good… interesting.'

'Aren't you enthusiastic about your cultural mission?'

'Indeed I am. I'm very pleased to be able to work here.'

I scanned the titles on the spines of the books on the shelf above his shoulder. Meanwhile he was looking at my list of duties.

'…but you don't have to make the coffee.'

'That's a relief, as I don't know how to anyway.'

'And now perhaps we could discuss your other duties over a beer.'

'I don't drink beer.'

'You can drink anything you like.'

'I don't drink anything you like,' I replied coolly and disdainfully, though I forced a smile to try to tone down the discourtesy of my response.

'Right, then.' Jermák's face showed no emotion as he headed for his desk. Halfway there he turned round. 'Then get to work!'

# 3

I TRUDGED HOME along the hard cement paths of the City Park, exhausted by a working day of a length unprecedented in my life. I looked up only rarely, just in case I should see someone I knew coming, I'd have time to get out of their way. As I crossed the threshold of our building, I thought I had now definitively deprived myself of the chance of anything more happening to me that day. I cast a passing glance at our post box.

My surname consists of two physicists' names, one Italian, the other French, both closely associated with the phenomenon of electricity. I have to credit my grandmother for this piece of creative thinking, which ensures that my acquaintances always have something to ask me about. I try to avoid situations which might require me to introduce myself using my full name; even the post box gives only my initials, and 'Jerne' is sufficient for the postman. I opened the flap and a longish envelope fell to the ground with POLSKA stamped boldly on it. When I inspected it somewhat more closely, I realized that this was a letter I had myself written two weeks earlier to Edward Leszczycki, in Poland. *Gone away, return to sender.*

I opened the envelope and as I slowly made my way up the stairs, I read the letter. This is what I had written to Edward Leszczycki, a fortnight earlier, at 2.00 in the morning, in Budapest.

*Dear Edward,*

*You will perhaps recall that when you went away I said I would be staying, and mocked you for returning to Eastern Europe. Imagine! Now I'm here too! The only difference is that I am resident in East-Central Europe. But I think we are both equally fortunate.*

*I could not say no to my Grandmother's summons. She came to visit me and spent days trying to convince me to return. She kept telling me what exciting things can happen when you are with Hungarians. She was right. After a long absence, I have now been back in Hungary for two months and I can confirm that nowhere else is life so interesting.*

*The reason I was reminded of you was that I remembered one of our discussions, about the nature of bureaucrats. We debated at length what they should be compared to, having agreed at the outset that if we could determine what kind of familiar creatures they resembled, we would understand how we should deal with them and thus deprive them of their mystique and air of invulnerability.*

*I averred that they reminded me of human beings, those possessed of autistic personalities in particular. I have nothing against those suffering from autism; I was merely recalling something I had read, that bureaucrats become upset if anything disturbs their routine. You countered that we should let autistic folk be, as some of them are astonishingly intelligent, whereas if we dealt with bureaucrats as if they were mentally retarded, our efforts would be crowned with success.*

*I apologize if I am boring you by reigniting this debate but I had to tell you this much at least. I think, Edward, we were both right. This clearly articulated theory is of enormous benefit to me in my everyday life.*

*In all other respects it's very good here. Many things are happening to me. For example, today I had an interview for a job at a publisher's. It looks as though I'll be employed there as copy-editor and proofreader. I would be responsible for matters of style and spelling, which is amusing because, although I spoke a great deal in this language up to the age of fourteen, I really am no expert.*

*The editor-in-chief is called Norma-Elektra; I'm utterly serious. The cruelty of parents is sometimes staggering: burdening someone with the name of two tragic heroines is surely a step too far. And indeed: she never smiles. But she did promise that they also offer opportunities to publish literature, particularly the efforts of up-and-coming young writers. So the firm would be prepared to publish my stories, provided they are 'up to scratch'. It's something they feel they owe to their permanent staff.*

*I hope my letter finds you well. Do you remember Winterwood at all? Let me know your full postal address!*

*Your friend, J. V. Ampere*

Well, yes. Even after all those years of English education, I still write in this effusive vein. I scrunched up the letter and threw it in the bin.

Winterwood. That's where I spent the most impressionable years of my life and consciously prepared for my deep cover, one that would satisfy both me and my surroundings: the writing of stories. Winterwood is a small and undistinguished college in a small town in the south of England. My Grandmother sent me there because she had heard on the grapevine that the very reincarnations of the Brontë sisters taught there and that it was therefore perfect for an aspiring story writer. I must admit that Grandma was a conscientious guardian who left no stone unturned to ensure that I become a well-educated corpse.

And can there be a more ideal place than England? All that wealth of accumulated experience! Thanks to the international character of the student body I learnt how to swear in French and I have ever since vented the frustrations occasioned by minor irritants in this language, as I don't like to utter obscenities openly. So I sometimes say: 'what a load of Lacan'; 'a positive pack of Derrida', and, if I stub my toe on a piece of furniture I exclaim: 'Foucault!' I could go on and on about all the practical skills I acquired, but naturally I also strove to gain theoretical knowledge, too, at this institution.

In general I stayed in the library until closing time and at the weekends I lay on my bed devouring the monologues of water rats and moles, the braggadocio of toads, the heroic deeds of daredevil house mice, the puns of chess pieces, the adventures of irrepressible redheads, the tragic fate of orphans, the mystical stories of kobolds and hobgoblins. And then there were the countless distinctive rabbits...

In the end I wrote my dissertation on *The Manifestation of the Rabbit in British Children's Literature, with Special Reference to the Victorian and Edwardian Era*, discussing, among others, the rabbits of Beatrix Potter, Lewis Carroll and A. A. Milne, but also including more anonymous figures, who might have cropped up only as elder rabbit, for example.

My supervisor was unsympathetic to my topic. First of all she took great glee in pointing out the fact that A. A. Milne's cult work was written in 1926, hence the authoritarian rabbit figure in it was not Edwardian but Georgian. The woman was an expert on bears, and since she had read somewhere that it was the Finno-Ugrians' custom to hold bear feasts, she suggested that my topic should be the brown-furred predator, saying that I might even have had personal experience of the bear cult. However, I had no such memories, since in Hungary, where I had spent a significant part of my childhood, there are none of these honey-pawed creatures to be found, quite apart from the fact that such a topic would have involved dealing with that absolute blockhead Winnie the Pooh, who simply makes me want to retch.

The rabbit is a dull-witted, foul-smelling and lascivious animal that appears in stories as a flesh and blood character possessed of human frailties, not as some idiot stuffed with sawdust. I would be very glad if everyone would at last admit that rabbits are just as fearless and venturesome as ordinary domestic rodents – indeed, they have far more complex personalities. I don't deny that by virtue of their size mice enjoy something of an advantage, but one must not underestimate the natural endowments of rabbits either, as these can be inestimable for the purposes of character building. The conception of my work was in fact based on just such attributes.

So: Edward Leszczycki had moved. No matter. He never replied to letters anyway.

# part II

## 4

BY THE FOURTH DAY I felt quite at home in my new workplace. All things considered I was happy to spend one-third of my day in that dark, cramped but well-heated room. The work offered exactly as much of a challenge as I wanted from life. First conjugation or second? Gerund or participle? Hyphenated or not? Comma, colon or semicolon? These were the problems that filled my universe and I felt a genuine sense of excitement when, after half an hour of steadily waning attention, the parched wordscape suddenly offered a juicy spelling mistake or a mouth-watering misprint. In the course of weeding out the texts I sometimes even had the chance to compose some trenchant dialogs for my animal tales.

I well recall that on the Thursday of my first week at work Norma-Elektra tapped on the frosted glass of the office.

'Jerne, there's a young man outside. He says he is an old friend of yours.'

I wondered who could possibly make such a claim, but by then Somi had already made his way into the room, accompanied by the sweetish smell that hung about his person. Yes, indeed.

Between the ages of six and fourteen we had both been fashioned by the school system into what we are today. The last time I heard, years ago, he was fronting Coitus Interruptus.

'Hiya, Jerke!' he said with a broad smile.

I didn't really mind the brazen diminutive, the humour of which derived from the phonetic similarity between my name and the term for young goats and lambs in Hungarian, but I did find it rather tiresome. Raising my eyebrows, I asked what he was doing here. He didn't need asking twice:

'I met your mother the other day, or rather the other night, waiting for a taxi. I said hello auntie, and she looked at me as if she was about to bite my head off. Then I saw she was with this guy twenty or thirty years younger, about our age, and my jaw fell. Now, I'm not saying your mother isn't still a bit of alright, her looks and figure are just like when we were still playing in the sandpit. How does she do it? Facelift? Botox?'

'She drinks human blood.'

'Ha ha. Nice one. Anyhow, she told me where you are working, some publisher with a line in self-help books. She didn't know its name, just the street you walk to every morning.'

'You were just passing by?'

'You got it. Just passing by, in no particular hurry, window shopping…'

'There are stores of every kind here. There's a seeds vendor, an umbrella repairer…'

'Yeah, and then I suddenly saw this brass plaque in a doorway, Elektra and Co., Publishers. I thought I'd drop in, as I'm in pretty lousy shape anyway and I could do with a few books on therapeuting my psyche. So what's new? What do you do all day in this hole?'

'I read.'

'Sounds good. Your mother said you write, too.'

That did make me sound truly versatile.

'True enough.'

'What kind of stuff do you write?'

'Animal tales.'

'Sounds good too. I am myself more of a lyrical bent. Did you know I write the band's songs? Of course, I have the highest literary standards.'

'Of course.'

'Read me one of your stories, just so I get a sense of your style.'

Not a letter or phone call for years and now, out of the blue, he wants to hear my stories. One of many reasons for my disinclination to do this was that I still had a vivid memory of assault and battery after I made a critical remark about Saint-Exupéry's deathless hero and Somi leapt at my throat howling 'Don't you dare fuck with the Little Prince!' And all I'd had the temerity to say was that the above-mentioned creature was a repulsive cretin. I still say that it's pretty pathetic that someone in his thirties imagines he is a little prince (I'm referring to the author).

'So, let's hear something!' Somi urged.

'Before we take such a step without due care, I want to ask what you think of Mole.'

'Which mole?'

'That Krtek, the mole that's longing for a pair of dungarees with pockets.'

'Smart guy.'

This at least sounded reassuring. I've had it up to the back teeth with animal heroes who spout sententious maxims. Even that shabby fox, the one that says 'You've tamed me, so now you must care for me,' or something of the sort, I would gladly punch in the gut. At least Krtek keeps quiet, at most uttering inarticulate little sounds. It's a little daft, though this reflects more his lack of experience as an animal. Whereas the Kenneth Grahame type of mole that the Anglo-Saxons know and love is endowed with the naivety of human beings.

'It's a rabbit. I mean, my animal. It's a rabbit.'

'The hero is a rabbit?'

'Yes. It's called Initiative.'

'What? You've got a degree in English or something? It really pisses me off when you parade your knowledge of languages. Why can't it have a proper Hungarian name?'

'The moment you start calling your band Megszakított Közösülés, I'll call the rabbit Kezdeményezőkészség, and not before.'

'OK, take it easy. No need to take offense. You're right, it adds to the mystique. As far as the kids are concerned, you might just as well call one of the girl rabbits Necrophilia.'

'Krafft-Ebing and Havelock Ellis at your fingertips, eh?'

'Who are they?'

'Never mind. Anyhow, in my stories these animals roam wild and free, gratifying their unbridled desires.'

'Do they screw?'

'Somi! It's a children's book!'

'Sorry. It was that bit about unbridled desires.'

'Let's change the subject…'

'Let's have the story!'

Jermák peered in through the glass and then tapped on it.

'Jerne! Are you ready with that piece I gave you three hours ago?'

The heaviness of this hint was obvious even to Somi.

'OK, I'll be off. It was good to have a sensible conversation with someone. Why don't you come to one of our gigs sometime? I'll call you, right? When I know when and where exactly we're playing.'

'Jerne, you do know that these are working hours?' came Jermák's voice from outside.

'Who is that slab of vomit?' Somi inquired.

'And Co.'

'So that's why he's such a stirrer. I hope Elektra sometimes tells him where to get off.'

'We can but hope.'

'Listen. How about going out tonight? We could talk about the good old days.'
'OK. What time?'
'7.00. In the playground, by the climbing frame.'

# 5

AS I HAVE already mentioned, in those days I was still alive and able to enjoy the taste of everything. As a result, I ate often. I ate for the sake of the taste, because when I was really hungry I'd just guzzle it down. It would have been a vain hope to imagine that Grandma, like one of those archetypal grandmothers, would be ready with my supper when I came home after a hard day's work. When the desire came upon me, I always had to fend for myself.

Exhausted after the day's labors, I was slicing tomatoes, with Grandma sitting beside me painting her toenails. I sometimes felt she had a social dependency problem, as she was always seeking out my company and wanting to talk with me.

'I dreamt of Móric Jókai,' she said suddenly with a painful sigh. 'I can't forget Móric. A hundred years pass, a hundred and fifty, and still I am unable to forget.'

Nothing was going to make me ask her about her dream, as I knew the script inside out. Grandma often dreamed of the Hungarian novelist active in the second half of the nineteenth century known as Mór Jókai and regarded as a great storyteller, from whose inexhaustible imagination tales of action and romance welled forth in an endless stream. I continued chopping the vegetables.

'Do you know what I dreamed?'

'I do,' I replied but I could see that honesty was not going to be any use here.

'How could you possibly know? I'm going to tell you. There he stood, in his coat of black velvet, his violet-blue eyes smiling for no one but me. I drew closer, mesmerized by his glance. I quickened my pace, so I could hold him tight all the sooner and sink my teeth into the delicate folds of his neck. And then of course the vision vanished and I woke up.'

It would have been a shame to miss out on this interesting dream. I knew what was coming next: Róza Laborfalvi.

'That insufferable Laborfalvi! She never let anyone near him. I mean, women,' Grandma went on.

Not even Grandma.

'Not even me.'

Because she was jealous.

'Because she was jealous. After all, she was an old woman compared with Móric. And I, whenever I went, was young and beautiful. In vain did I, an ardent admirer of his work, seek an audience with the great writer. The maid would go in, then her ladyship would come out and say "My husband is at work on a novel. He is not receiving anyone today, young lady, I'm sorry".'

The hell she was sorry.

'The hell she was sorry. She just wouldn't let me see him.'

'Why didn't you try after he was widowed? When he was lonely. After Laborfalvi and before Bella Nagy,' I said, trying to be constructive.

'Have you taken leave of your senses? I wouldn't touch an old man with a bargepole. Don't you think, Jerne, that it's repulsive the way elderly men drag their wizened bodies with such pride through the streets and squares and other public spaces? No one over forty should be allowed to live, and yet there they all are, everywhere… But I'm worried about you, Jerne, worried that's how you'll end up.'

'How?'

'Unless you start sucking blood soon, there'll be hell to pay. It's in your blood, as it were, but what would really motivate you is if you died. Until then you won't care how the days pass.'

'I do want to die, Grandma, but not just yet.'

'No need to actually die. I didn't say you should die. All I want is to see you become as strong, clever and gorgeous a vampire as I am. That reminds me: have I shown you my business cards?'

'You've had new business cards printed?'

'Well, you know how it is. In the business world it is essential to have top-quality, well-designed business cards that misinform my partners in an appropriate manner. Here, look!' Grandma took a slim little wallet from her evening bag. 'There are twenty different ones in this set, on heavy paper, in Sacré Cœur font. I spent hours racking my brains trying to come up with twenty new names. I'll soon have to recycle some of the old ones.'

'Magnificent. But what's this? Where it says under your name: Finno-Ugrian Vampire?'

'Those are for restricted use. In case I should have dealings with my kind.'

'But there's no such thing as a Finno-Ugrian vampire. Finno-Ugrian is a linguistic or ethnographic term. What's wrong with Hungarian vampire?'

'What a vulgar notion! Just think how some arrogant Anglo-Saxon vampire would react if I presented myself as a Hungarian vampire. There'd be a polite nod. "I see. And where is Hungary exactly? Budapest or Bucharest?" But Finno-Ugrian: that arouses instant respect and lends me an aura of the exotic.'

'And that's it?'

'That's it.'

'I thought for a moment you had some patriotic obsession.'

'Nothing pathological. Although I must admit I do like living here. The Hungarians' gene pool is suitably variegated and as a result their external appearance is incredibly varied in form and color and, frequently, rather attractive. Many of them are good-looking and appetising. Nowhere is the food, if I may be permitted to express myself in such a crude manner, so boring as in countries with a homogeneous population. You can take my word for it. In such places people resemble each other like two slices of buttered bread, like two peas in a pod or like two pieces of smoked herring. Do you get my meaning? Are my similes suitably graphic?'

'Yes.'

Grandma began to inspect the items on my plate more closely. 'What are you eating? What is that awful stuff?'

'Salad.'

'That won't give you eternal youth. How many times have I told you, Jerne, to listen to your grandmother. If you want something really nutritious, order a pizza delivery boy!'

She had indeed told me a thousand times and had continued to hope against hope that I would one day give up my light suppers and have a sweaty delivery boy or girl instead.

# 6

I STOOD BY the climbing frame, waiting for Somi, and my eight-year-old self appeared before my eyes, my sweating hands sliding along the metal tubing as terror gripped me by the throat and then, suddenly, I lay helpless on the gravel. Because Somi had said that if I didn't dare do a handstand on top of the climbing frame, I was a weakling. It was a word he had just picked up from some action film. I did dare but I just couldn't manage it. We'd been playing in the same playground since we were three but we were not yet close, as Somi belonged to a sandcastle-demolishing gang, whose proclivities – since I dreamed of constructing the Bavarian king Ludwig II's neo-Gothic pile in sand – aroused my definite disapproval.

Then, one stifling hot summer's day, when all the other children were away on vacation or at camp, we had to fall back on each other's company. I participated in Somi's first frog dissection: that was the breakthrough. I soon regretted my action and not since the age of nine have I bragged about having been the one to hand him the tweezers and the boning knife. But we remained comrades in arms until I discovered there was a children's library nearby. Of course, we also went to the same school for a while, but Grandma soon packed me off to the private college.

'Hiya. Been waiting long?' Somi had arrived.

'I just got here. I see they haven't painted the climbing frame since.'

'Why? Do they re-paint playground equipment regularly in England?'

'I don't know. I didn't visit playgrounds.'

'I do sometimes. But only at night. That's when the swings are free.'

'Me too, I always went on the swings at night.'

'You were always different. You were the only one from our class to walk out of *Pinocchio* in the middle of the show. I suspected even then you'd be a somebody.'

'But I'm not anybody.'

'But you *will* be a somebody. You've been educated abroad, you're a writer, and all that stuff.'

'It's only been a few days since I offered my first stories to the publisher.'

'It's bound to work out. You came first in the story-writing competition in fourth grade.'

'That was the story-reading competition in second grade. In fourth I was an also-ran. Despite submitting a plagiarized version of 'The Stork Caliph' from the *One Thousand and One Nights.*'

'Were you disqualified?'

'They didn't even notice. They just didn't like it.'

'I had no luck either in the talent competitions at school. And yet here I am. All I need at each gig is ten more people than turned up to the one before and I'll be a star in no time. It's definitely on the cards: the pubs we play are always packed.'

'What's your instrument?'

'I only do vocals now. At first I played lead guitar as well but I realized I couldn't give my best if I try to do two things at once. They put me out front because I like being seen. But at the moment no one is looking. Though the situation is improving from gig to gig. Hey, won't you have something to drink?'

'You mean alcohol?' I asked in alarm.

'Of course. But not 100 degrees proof. Something distilled from grain or fruit,' Somi explained. 'Barley, hops, wheat. Otello grape or Beszterce plum.'

'I don't consume alcoholic beverages.'

'No? So how are you going to become a writer?'

'I don't want to become a great writer. Just a little story writer.'

'Doesn't mean you couldn't have a little drink. Just to be sociable.'

'No way. Alcohol does me harm. It makes me cheerful and nice.'

'Right. Then you'll have something else. Come on, let's go,' said Somi, and we set off for the lights in the distance.

7

I WAS MAKING my third attempt to eliminate a particularly elaborate Germanism and meanwhile conjuring up a graphic and detailed scenario of what it would be like if I became a published author. First I would pick up the volume (fresh and hot!) from the printer, linger over the title page, then flip through the pages that bore my words. I'd swell with pride as I reflected on the path I'd traversed since the age of five, when I couldn't even

read and even wrote the letter N back to front. Initially, I would
have the media monitoring service check for reviews. Within the
next few months a couple of notices would appear, one of them
pointing out that behind the clodhopping animal stories there
lurked a pithy critique of society, and I would be transfixed with
joy: this is exactly what I'd hoped to read! Later, once the hubbub
around my book had died down, I would make weekly visits to
the better bookstores, those that stocked quality literature and
offered browsers tea and coffee. I would check out the youth
section, caressing with my eyes the spine of my books of animal
stories, and sometimes buy the odd copy, just to show that it
was selling, that it was something for the true lover of literature.

An idle fancy. I gave a profound sigh (ah!) and stared dreamily
out of the window. At that moment I felt a light touch on my arm.
I looked up. Norma-Elektra gave a delicate smile and motioned
me to follow her. We sat down in her office facing each other.

'Would you like some coffee?'

'No, thank you.'

'I would.' She sat down but immediately leapt to her feet again
and hurried over to the coffee machine. 'I have read your stories.'

'And what do you think?'

'We agreed, didn't we, that our publishing house would put
them out.'

'If they were up to scratch.'

'Indeed. I will be straight with you. Your stories cannot be
published in this form.'

'Why not?'

'You want reasons?'

'If you'd be so kind.'

'Right.' She stood with her back to me, busying herself
with the coffee machine as she explained: 'You're a very gifted
storyteller, no question. I also appreciate that you feel story
writing to be your vocation. There are so many for whom it's
just a sideline...' Gurgling sounds began to issue from the coffee

machine.'…and yet they still manage to write better stories. Even so, I sense something stirring within you. But these stories are not yet ripe for publication.' She returned to her desk and pressed the manuscript firmly into my hands. 'See? I've marked in purple the sections that simply won't do and added notes in the margin.'

'Darling!' Jermák stuck his head round the door. 'I have to go now, I might be late getting back. Don't wait up for me.'

'Fine, see you when I see you,' said Elektra and held her smile until Jermák's head disappeared.

'What won't do, for example?' I wanted specifics.

'Now, let's not dwell on the negative side! I'd rather point to all the good things. Dialogue: that's certainly your forte. And spare, simple sentences. But your descriptions are limp and lifeless.'

'Ah.'

'But that's not the biggest problem. It's these rabbits, foxes, wolves, polecats, moles and gophers – they're all cynical and evil.'

'Of course they are. That's why the title is *Rotten Animals*.'

'Jerne, this really will not do. Moral content is required.'

'A pithy critique of society?'

'What?'

'Do you think the book embodies a pithy critique of society?'

'You mean this?' Elektra stabbed a finger at my manuscript with disgust. 'You should at least have indicated who was good and who was bad. A child can't be expected to know.'

'Wasn't it interesting?'

'Very interesting. But I'm not publishing it.'

'Why not?'

'Because it's my publishing house. Or rather, ours. But I'm quite certain that my co-owner shares my moral values.'

My lips must have curled downwards, for she added:
'Just make the changes. Then we'll see.'

# part III

## 8

*Now, this is the bottle. In it is something called Pálinka or schnapps. Little reader, I hope you will not consume anything like this as long as you live. This is poison. Just like vodka, rum and whisky. These are what are called hard liquor. So hard, they knock people out and kill them.*

I WAS SITTING at my desk in the office. It was past 10.00, yet this was all I had managed to cobble together by way of moral content and even this I had lifted from an Alcoholics Anonymous leaflet. I could see that what I had was slim pickings, but then how could someone from the forces of darkness have insight into the ethical values of humanity? Good job they didn't want to incorporate a little dance theory into the work – that was something I knew even less about. Quite apart from the fact that my sympathies were with the depraved gang of lesser and greater predators every inch of the way. I am quite insensible to goodness. On the other hand, I did at least know that the consumption of alcohol was a sensitive issue for human beings.

I really don't crave literary immortality – I will achieve eternal life through my bloodline as a vampire. All I want is to see my work in print. Is that so much to ask? Why are my carefully-crafted stories less worthy than the subjective coffee-house scribblings of poets about their momentary physical and mental states? I'm acutely aware that only the select few can write lyric poetry, but in the end everyone can write prose, so it is to these products of the spirit that the most stringent criteria must be applied; but if there is anyone that deserves to be admitted to the hallowed status of story writer, it's me.

At such difficult times the example of Hans Christian Andersen always hovered before my eyes. Hans Christian Andersen never gave up. When he was young he wanted to be a ballet dancer: he was advised that was not a good idea. Later he wanted to be a singer and actor: after a few roles as an extra, he was sent packing from the theater. Then, and later, too, in fact all the time, he tried to make it as a poet: he was ridiculed (especially when he recited his poetry himself). He also failed as a playwright: his plays were howled off the stage. In the end he wrote a few dreadful novels. This fact had two consequences for the history of European culture: a young man called S. Kierkegaard was so enraged by them that he was impelled to write his first serious piece, an extensive critique of Andersen, and the novels enjoyed Europe-wide success, laying the foundations for their author's future and thus allowing him to pursue his story writing. Today no respectable children's bedroom would be without his tales of sadomasochism.

As for me, I wrote my first animal story while I was at elementary school. It was called *Good old Fido, the life and adventures of a simple dog*. I showed it to our school teacher. She encouraged me to pursue this path, though without ever forgetting that the story writer is always trying to navigate between the Scyllas and Charybdis of the sea of words. The sweet, honeyed song of the sirens of sentimentalism can easily tempt him to run aground and that certainly means the end of the story. But careful composition will enable him to turn a deaf ear to the alluring songs and he will thus be able to steer his vessel into the safe harbour that he seeks. 'Let the wax of concision drip steadily into your ears so you avoid being shipwrecked!' she advised.

But this is not the only thing that matters. Take animal stories, for example. At bottom, there are two kinds of animal tale. One is about humanoids in animal form, who wear clothes, have a social life and are endowed with human traits. The other type tries to present animals as animals. This is clumsy because few of us are able to truly appreciate what it feels like to be an animal. Yet all one needs is a high degree of empathy. And let us not forget that we are all inclined to make furry and cuddlesome little animals into positive heroes, and no less furry but less cuddlesome – even scaly and slimy – animals into negative ones. And yet all this is illusory: the whole sorry crew is narrow-minded, lacking in moral qualities, with nothing on their minds except consumption and reproduction. Anthropomorphism is the death-knell of the imagination, I thought, and with a thick red pencil crossed out the paragraph with two befuddled weasels wheezing along behind Initiative as he lugged a carrier bag full of foraged turnips. I was back to square one, inspiration was beyond reach; I needed to find something new to fill my life.

I yawned. It was pitch-black outside, a slimy autumn rain clinging to every object in sight. I'm not going to leave here tonight, I decided; who's going to notice if I spend the night here? I made myself up a bed in the smaller of the two rooms, the one where I worked, pushing the eight available chairs together to make a reasonably comfortable structure. I left the door slightly ajar, so that a little light would filter in from the other room, which looked out on to the street.

I laid my tired head on the faux leather of the office furniture and fell asleep at once. I dreamt that I lost my virginity at the age of sixteen, but what was truly frightening in my dream was that I ate some unwashed cherries, went blind, and filthy rodents jumped on my face. I was therefore not too sorry to be woken by the jingle of keys. I am not, frankly, the most courageous of folk, so at first I just laid low with my eyes closed, hoping that if this was a break-in, the thief would take whatever he wanted and if at all possible not even notice my presence. But I then realized that, judging by the sounds, the visitor had taken off his coat. I doubted that anyone who had gained unauthorized entry would go to such trouble. Noiselessly I slid off my night-time perch and crept slowly to the door on all fours to see what I could.

When I caught sight of the intruder, I was about to stand up and say hello, but stopped myself, wondering whether my presence might not be taken exception to. At this point, however, the figure went over to the little washbasin in the corner and by the light of the moon I could clearly see that what he was trying to remove from his face was nothing other than blood! He rinsed out his mouth and the light from the street fell across his face. The voluptuous, cruel smile made me give an involuntary shudder. Wow. Every interjection that came to mind (Jesus Christ, Good God, Christ Almighty, Jesus, Joseph and Mary) was connected with the cultural domain of Christianity and hence not appropriate to cross the lips of someone of my kind. I had to content myself with opening my eyes very wide. There was no doubt: my boss is a vampire. My boss, too, is a vampire.

Jermák took a few more minutes to clean up: he massaged some baby soap into his hirsute chest, splashed some water on it, then used the tiny hand towel hanging by the basin to rub down his somewhat chubby, snow-white body (to think I'd wiped my hands in that! – I shuddered). He put on a clean shirt and then took a swig from the hip-flask he had taken out of his pocket. He locked the cupboard, slid the key into the folds of the floor cloth, then picked up his things and hurriedly left the apartment.

I slipped back on to my improvised bed. I hummed and hawed, shaking my head: this disgusting world is full of vampires. Poor

Norma-Elektra. I wondered if she knew? After this I didn't dare fall asleep. I was worried I wouldn't wake up in time and it would have been awkward in the extreme if anyone found out that I had observed Jermák washing blood off his body. Hmm. My superior was a bloodsucker. I weighed up my chances of survival and came to the conclusion that if I could potter around for eight hours a day here and be paid the minimum I needed to survive, I'd have absolutely nothing to complain about. And I don't.

As soon as the sun came up, I stole over to the other room to survey the scene. I grabbed the key out of the wet floor cloth and unlocked the cupboard. It was full of junk: cigars, pipe tobacco, old photographs, books, letters, shiny little stones and a small locked casket whose contents I took no interest in whatsoever. So these are the accoutrements of a vampire? It was the shirt that most interested me; I went to inspect it very carefully. Blood. No doubt about it. The collar had been soiled by the vital sap where it must have dripped from his mouth. All the same, there was a ten per cent chance, I thought, that he had simply been slapped viciously across the face.

# 9

EVEN AFTER taking a turn in the refreshing dawn air, I was able to bask in the smug glow of seemingly having arrived early. I hoped Norma-Elektra would take note of how reliable a member of her workforce I was. I spent all day with my eyes glued to Jermák. He was tired and unshaven. I found it hard to imagine how someone so physically unattractive could belong to the noble vampire race. Now, while I cannot boast of exceptional beauty myself, my typically aristocratic nose lends a certain dignity to my features. I could detect no signs of external damage to his face, only that expansive glow of satisfaction that spreads across

Grandma's face whenever she has worked her way through an entire boardroom. In the end it was the mystery shrouding Jermák's age that convinced me that here was no ordinary mortal. I used every trick in my book to try to find out how old he might be. These amounted to going over to his desk and asking him:

'Excuse me, how old are you?'

'Thirty,' he replied, giving me a stare.

Anyone can say that. Very suspicious.

After a day devoted to observing the office vampire, I went home to the other one. She was stretched out on the daybed in a satin housecoat, applying cold compresses to her calves.

'What's up, Grandma?'

'Just look at this! I've turned black and blue in five places.'

'Oh dear. Who did this to you?'

'Well, I was coming home at dawn, and who the hell feels like climbing five flights, my feet were really sore in my high heels, and there's no elevator in this wretched building, of course. I thought I'd batwing it up to the fifth floor, and the caretaker turned on me with a broom on the fourth, and kept hitting me until his strength gave out.'

'You mustn't be surprised. Not everyone is fond of bats.'

'I see. So you think he should have battered me to death?'

'I'm not saying that. Just that I appreciate why he might have been alarmed.'

'What empathy! Your grandmother almost ends her days as a dead bat and you just nod in agreement.'

'Oh, come on, Gran, you wouldn't give in so easily.'

'What else could I expect of you, you, in whose veins only traces of vampire blood flow, in dribs and drabs. Your father and your mother…'

I waited expectantly for her to continue, but Grandma stopped short. I hoped that one day she would swear at me in such comprehensive terms that she would include a reference to my mother and I would discover what sort of creature she had been. For I could entertain only the faintest hope that I, too, had been born of a mother. The box in which I had arrived, a few days old, at Grandma's was plastered with the following labels: 'EXPRESS, REGISTERED, PERISHABLE, FRAGILE. Contents: grandchild.' I had lain curled up on wood shavings, reeking of poppy-seed tea. I will probably never be able to thank Grandma enough for taking me in, even though at first she had wrapped me up again and wanted to return me to the sender, but the postman would not accept me without the sender's name on the certificate of posting. She fed me and clothed me and always defended me when the need arose. For example, when at the age of twelve I had a nightmare in which Lenin and the Resolutions of the Party Committee came for me (figurines in the shape of the *Erlkönig*), she didn't let me be taken, she bared her teeth and everything. They got cold feet.

'And where were you, Jerne, last night? Surely you didn't… suck blood?'

'No.'

'I thought as much.'

'Why? I could have done.'

'You don't say. That'll be the day!'

Clearly, Grandma considered me an incompetent sucking pig. I trudged off to my room and stared dully into the lights of the metropolis.

## 10

'SOMI, are you still unwell? Has the walk not exhausted you too much?' I asked. 'When I rang in the afternoon, your brother said you were laid up.'

'I'm on the mend. I wouldn't have come otherwise,' Somi replied cheerfully, as he tried to knock off the cap of the beer bottle on the seat of the park bench with repeated blows of his clenched fist. 'I had an old flame visiting, I always spend my time recovering from Spanish flu with her.'

He managed to get the cap off the bottle and took a swig of the beer, which we had just bought from the all-night ABC nearby, a store with a pricing policy that Somi called night-and-daylight robbery. I picked up a newspaper there and now that we had finally sat down on one of the park benches at the edge of the boating lake, I began to browse the advertisements.

'Look at this!' I said, pointing to one. 'Vacancy for five conceptual artists, immediate start. Beginners welcome. Salary: in due course.'

'Tempting offer,' Somi commented. 'But how come you're looking for a job? Not long ago you were happy in your place of work.'

'I am indeed happy. I don't deserve anything better. But I've always been interested in conceptual art.'

'Why not give it a try? It says beginners can have a go. It's one thing to be a story writer, but why couldn't you be a conceptual artist or an opera singer? Artists are versatile. As for me, I have my sights set on being a translator of literature. By the way, when did you say your stories were coming out?'

'Perhaps never.'

'No way. Hey, let's give the ducks one of our rolls. The dum-dums. Here they are exerting themselves even in the autumn.'

We broke up one of the rolls, which we had also bought in the ABC, into small pieces and threw them into the lake one at a time.

'Why shouldn't they publish them?' Somi continued, 'after all, you work in the publisher's, where the action is.'

'What planet are you living on? You think this is a matter of who you know? Standards in the publishing business are very high.'

'I never knew that. But I'm glad you've told me.'

'I did in fact rewrite the stories recently, and I'm just waiting to hear what they say.'

'Full steam ahead, then.' Somi threw the last piece of roll into the lake and reached for the bottle. 'Listen, Jerne, there's something I've been meaning to ask you for a long time...'

'Ask away.'

'Do you prefer boys or girls?'

'I really don't know,' I mused. 'Neither boys nor girls. I don't really like people.'

'I see. And animals?'

'Those I don't have any relations with at all.'

'Sun's up,' Somi reported. 'Breakfast time!'

We shared out the remaining rolls. I got two but didn't touch either. I watched the little white balls of dough swelling up in the water.

'But I'm glad we chucked those bits of roll in,' said Somi, his mouth full. 'Because by the time the ducks wake up, they'll have got thoroughly soaked and every bite will melt in their beaks. I'm suddenly inspired to write a song about what I'm feeling, but I think I'll have a nap first, before the dog walkers and joggers arrive. How about you?'

'I'm off to work. I haven't done any work for twelve hours. I'm beginning to miss it.'

'Up to you. But do ring me if you feel like having a walk again. It was a rewarding experience.'

'For me, too.'

I gave him a wave and set off.

# 11

THE REVISED VERSION of my manuscript, which I had handed in on Monday, was already lying on my desk. This time Elektra didn't even deign to reject it to my face. She came over only a few minutes before the end of the working day. She pulled up a chair and began, with a ravishing smile.

'So, have you come to terms with it?'

I repeated my Hans Christian Andersen mantra, which was particularly suited to the occasion.

'It's really important that one should be able to process one's setbacks,' my employer continued. 'Setbacks take you ahead. They light the way to success. If one pursues unattainable goals, one will be disappointed time and again. One has to retain one's sense of reality and formulate one's goals within the bounds of what can be achieved, adjusting them to one's experiences as one goes along. It is my firm belief that every young person has talent. But the realisation of certain goals needs an extended period of time, a great deal of experience, as well as a lot of practice. When you come to look back, in five or ten years' time, you will see that I only wanted the best for you by not letting your early efforts come before a wider public. The time will come when you will feel you have found your own voice and realize how unfortunate it would have been if you had allowed your juvenilia to cast a shadow over your non-existent renown.'

I frowned.

'Jerne, rejoice that I am about to offer you an opportunity to fulfil yourself. Listen!' She placed before me a little book with yellowing pages. 'This is a collection of folk tales, containing rarely anthologized stories. I found it in a second-hand bookstore. The name of a long-deceased publisher is on the cover, the editors, too, are long dead, so there will be nothing to pay for the rights. I spoke not long ago to another small publisher like us, who told me what unexpected success he'd had with a recent collection of folk tales. It's the kind of thing parents are always glad to buy. And why should Elektra and Co. miss out on publishing such tales, when we have a real expert on stories in our midst?'

'My stories...' I whimpered.

'Now at last you have a task you're cut out for. As these were originals, collected on the spot, they'll need some slight adjustments so that children will understand them. You'll leave out the dialect words, trim the bombast and rid the text of licentious turns of phrase, so that it will be simple and easy to digest. Well? What do you say? Isn't this an inspiring task? How do you like it?'

'I like it very much. Very much.'

'I knew you'd be pleased. But I beg of you: don't write things like "The fox was orally fixated all afternoon." There are so many foreign words in your stories, they'd make a four- or five-year-old drop stone dead. Hungarian, understood?'

'Understood.'

'So, get down to it, my girl. Give it your all!' Elektra said cheerily as she left the room and shortly thereafter the building.

'When you leave, make sure you lock up everything!' she trilled on her way out.

At times like this Hans Christian Andersen would only have given himself a shake like a wet dog and knelt effortlessly at the feet of another of his influential patrons. My stories, my wonderful, exciting, wise stories... And I, a qualified story writer, who had specialized in Children's Literature at Winterwood, completed courses on the classics of children's literature and the symbolism of the fairy tale, taken part in seminars on 'Walt Disney and the Schemata of the Traditional Tale' and 'The Joys and Difficulties of Story Writing' – all, all had been in vain. Now here I am, I've grown fond of my work, revel in inserting commas into the texts of 400-page yoga handbooks but this, the re-writing of folk tales, is one step too far. Why do I have to work at all? Probably even Hans Christian Andersen never had to do this kind of thing.

# 12

HARDLY HAD I WALKED into our building and the words 'rats, rats, rats' rang in my ears. As any mention of rodents and carrion-eating parasites is for me always directly associated with Grandma, I began to busy myself by the letter boxes to listen in on the conversation between the caretaker and one of the tenants, peppered with swear words and angry outbursts. A couple of minutes of this was enough for me to get the gist. I hurried upstairs and burst into our apartment.

A herd of rats was frolicking on the carpet, while two of the bigger ones were fighting it out over a large bone in the kitchen.

'I hope you don't mind them taking refuge here. The exterminators could be here any moment and I had to make sure they were somewhere safe,' Grandma said by way of welcome, baldly and without a hint of an apology.

'Grandma, you have frightened the caretaker's wife half to death with your creatures.'

'I have the right to keep whatever household pets I want.'

'Right. Well, you go and explain to her that these are your pets.'

'She is too stupid to understand.'

'It's you who are stupid. Not everyone delights in seeing slimy rats fattened on cat food popping up from the toilet bowl. She could have dropped dead from the sight.'

'That's what she said, eh?' Grandma said cockily.

'Yes. She was telling one of the old biddies that she never knew rats could climb so far up from the sewers.'

'Poppycock. They can get up to the ninth floor easily. Especially if they are as muscular and as well-fed as mine. Dear Mrs Caretaker might care to familiarize herself with the latest literature on the topic.'

'I do feel for her. Even I'm filled with dread when I see your creatures.'

'Well, you would be.'

I was five. I was standing in the yard with Grandma by the side of a Tyrannosaurus Rex-sized rat, which was picking about in the rubbish in a blasé manner.

'Rats are one of the vampires' friends,' Grandma instructed me. 'Give it a stroke!' she ordered.

I was disinclined to make friends with it and instead began to howl at the top of my voice, which meant that not only did the rat scurry away but the whole house came out on to the corridors, wondering if the arrogant beauty from the fifth floor was flaying her kid alive. And our cousin, the werewolf and the unavoidable bat were still to come.

'What do you mean "you would be"?'

'What else could I expect of you?'

'Well, now, here we go again. What the vampire is, and what it isn't. Just tell me what's on your mind, let it all hang out.'

'Stop bitching, my dear.'

'Why can't I be a real vampire?'

'But you can, of course you can.'

'But?'

'The family connection is not always enough. No offense, but someone like you, who has to be picked up off the floor even when you have a blood test… Well, you were hardly born into the purple. Would you even dare to make a wound?'

'Why shouldn't I?'

'Come on, then! Let's see you have a rat. Don't be scared, these won't run away, they're tame… Go on!'

'Have a rat?'

'Are there any well-fed young men to hand?'

'I have to start with a rat?'

'They're not my pigeon, as it were, but I saw a film where the hero just bolted them down one after the other with gusto, smacking his lips. Can't be bad.'

'I don't think I could even bear to touch one.'

'Well, then, there's nothing for it but to have a go on yourself.'

'What?'

'Do you want to do it with your teeth or with a razor blade?'

I wondered if I could keep the incredulity going. Why not, I thought, there's plenty of time.

'What?'

'Didn't you hear me?' Grandma snapped.

'Razor blade.'

Grandma opened the table drawer and gave me a packet of blades.

'Get on with it, my dear.'

'Here? With you watching?'

'It will stay within the family.'

I quickly unwrapped a blade. I clenched my teeth and with determined movements made three cuts on my left wrist. The blood came bubbling out in spurts, like icicles melting from the eaves.

'Right, let's bind it up!' Grandma took some gauze from the same drawer as the packet of blades. I was breathing heavily with the emotional effort and slid from the arm of the chair I was sitting on down on to the seat.

'Do vampires yearn for nirvana?' I asked.

Grandma mopped up the blood, sprinkled some medicinal talc on the wound and tied a pretty bow on the dressing.

'Jerne, you make me despair. If your great-grandfather were alive, he would be turning in his grave,' she said and pushed me in the direction of my room.

# part IV

## 13

THE NEXT DAY Jermák could not take his eyes off the dressing on my wrist, not for a moment. When Norma-Elektra hurried away to a meeting with some author, Jermák pulled up a chair and settled down by my desk.

'Can I see?'

'What?'

'Your wound.'

Three tiny scars were assiduously healing on my wrist and there was a danger that soon a whole flock of vampires would be snapping there with their teeth. Grandma had often warned me that open wounds were a serious danger because of what it would arouse in them – arouse in us.

'Is it still bleeding? Does it still hurt?'

'Why are you interested?'

'I can bring you something that will help it heal.'

'What? Bloodwort?'

'That too.'

'It's none of your business.'

'But honestly, if you need help of any kind, just say the

word. I'm thinking here not primarily about material, but rather spiritual assistance. If you want to have a talk with someone, say. Just tap on the glass, I'm there in the next room. Or we could, I don't know, have a coffee somewhere.'

'I'm not thirsty.'

'That's not why people have coffee. They have it in order to have it together. I feel responsible for you, as you are my employee, we work together. Your well-being is in my interest, too, it ensures effective work. Do you feel comfortable in your own skin?'

'I appreciate your concern, but even if I didn't, that would be a personal matter.'

'All right, all right. I don't want to push myself, not for the world, but a kind word from a fellow human being doesn't come amiss sometimes,' Jermák demurred, and continued to stare spellbound at the dressing. 'Oh, go on, please show me!' he begged and reached for my wrist. Horrified, I stuck my hand under the table.

'No need to feel ashamed.'

'I don't feel in the least ashamed, but it's none of your business.'

'Very well. You can go home now. It's 4.00 on Friday afternoon, no one's working. Just go home!'

He pushed the chair back and made for his room.

'But I have plenty of ideas...' he said, turning back in the doorway with a sly smile, '...for making you open up,' he added.

## 14

*Chapter III. A Few Grievances*

*'So you are of the opinion that I am a cynical animal,' the Gopher piped up suddenly, as he lit another cigar. The Mole gave a shudder, as until then he had been eyeing the valuable Rippl-Rónai hanging on the wall of the Gopher's drawing room.*

'Excuse me, what did you say?' he asked, somewhat moved, as he detected an element of annoyance in the Gopher's voice.

'Quite by chance I have learnt what you have been saying to folk in the Organic Garden. The Weasel was kind enough to tell me the way you recounted to a sizeable crowd how I had obtained that shady corner of the carrot field and allegedly mocked those who were worried about the family of rabbits on the verge of starvation,' the Gopher continued in an offended tone.

The Mole, for whom Zen had been his light and strength for many years, leaned back in his armchair and cleared his throat.

'I wonder if you might offer me a cigar?'

'Please help yourself,' said the Gopher, proffering his unnecessarily ornate cigar case.

The Mole took out a cigar, passed it under his nose, and lit up with relish.

'What would you say if we simply enjoyed our cigars?' he proposed.

The Gopher nodded and they both stared into the middle distance, wreathed in smoke. In a while it was again the Gopher who broke the silence.

'Tears come to my eyes, whenever I think of '48.'

'48?'

'1848, the Springtime of Nations.'

'Now why did you bring that up? Are you trying to provoke me? To let off some of your nationalist explosives?' the Mole asked louchely, between two puffs on his cigar.

'Don't be oversensitive, Mole,' said the Gopher in a friendly tone. 'All I'm suggesting is that we could celebrate this day in the Organic Garden, too. You are an intellectual animal, you could organize it.'

'Of course,' said the Mole casually. The smoke enveloped him softly.

'We could raise a statue to one of my ancestors, the one that leapt at the throat of one of the Emperor's soldiers. Some talented animal could make the cast.'

'You know my views on that score,' the Mole noted ominously.

'On what score? Let me think… Ah, I know. A flash of your eyes is enough to make me exercise self-criticism. Yes, perhaps this is a modest personality cult.'

'You're paranoid, Gopher,' the Mole said in a measured tone, because he had decided that he would not under any circumstances allow himself to be disconcerted today.

The Gopher stubbed out his half-smoked cigar, leaving it in the ashtray as he walked over to a low table. What sacrilege, thought the Mole, but said not a word.

'Paranoid? Perhaps. But now let's have a drink.'

'Anniversary? Birthday?'

'Let's call it that. Those are never in short supply. For example, only the other day I discovered that one of my sons from this year's litter has already made me a grandfather. The lad doesn't waste any time, does he?' the Gopher said with pride and took two clean glasses from the little cupboard under the table.

'Congratulations. You gophers are certainly very fecund,' said the Mole resignedly.

'But I'm now going to be honest with you, my dear Mole. I just want to get as drunk as an animal. This is my plan in the short term. I would be glad if you joined me.'

'Forgive me, Gopher, if I don't. Alcohol is so calorie rich that it would ruin my diet. I'm sure you know how those alcoholic drinks make you put on weight…'

WELL, THERE YOU ARE. I've gone pretty much the whole hog on this anti-alcohol business. And this has happened because in practice this was the one ethical issue that I felt I could take on. I couldn't get within even spitting distance of the rest. I don't know what makes someone evil – for me evil is the normal way of life.

I was listening to the radio, which instead of officially announcing winter, was excitedly broadcasting announcements that snow had fallen. Every half hour the populace had its attention drawn to the advisability of laying in food, in the form of tinned and dry goods and bottled water, so that a possible interruption in supplies would not cause any distress. Distressed myself, I bent over my manuscript. No entirely proper fall of snow was going to get me upset. As if we were living in the tropics and a fall of snow in early December were such a curiosity! Around 5.00 a.m. a bat tapped on the windowpane. I opened the window and let it in. It was Grandma. Inspired by the decrease in traffic occasioned by the blocked roads and hence the lower concentration of carbon dioxide, she had been hovering above the city since darkness fell.

'I've spied out where the snow-sweepers are concentrated.' Despite the exercise in the fresh air, Grandma's face remained as pallid as ever. 'There'll be no hold-ups in my supplies if there are any snowdrifts.'

She gave a shake, splattering me with drops of water.

'Can you hear, my dear? It's the phone.'

I made no move.

'All right, I'll get it.' Grandma hurried out into the hallway. She was soon back in my room, and spoke into my ear.

'It's a man. I wonder who it could be. Do you know?'

'He didn't introduce himself?'

'No.'

I picked up the receiver.

'Hello. Jerne Voltampere.'

'Hiya, it's me, Jermák. I was just wondering if you had time to come and have a drink, the snow is so wonderful. We should meet. Important business. I want to talk to you about your stories.'

'Ah.'

'Do you mean you don't even drink tea, or that you have no time? Why would you lie?'

'But I really do have no time. But I suppose I could break off for a while. Where shall we meet?'

'I'll show you a place.'

'OK. I'll be down in the square, by the office.'

'Fine. See you in twenty minutes.'

Grandma stood behind me throughout.

'Well, how do you intend to increase your allure?'

'I don't want to increase my allure.'

'Then he won't like you.'

'Why should he? I don't want him to.'

'Why should he?! Don't be such a hothead! Choosing men is fine. We'll go halves. There's enough of them to sink a battleship, and it's well worth starting with them. First of all, they can grow to quite a size, which means they have plenty of blood. And then they're made up of so many attractive parts that what I would absolutely love to do is take them to pieces, and then, when I've sucked out all their blood, I'd just have my fill of looking at them. Bee-stung lips, nut-brown or olive-green or ice-blue eyes, thick, arched eyebrows, noble noses, necks with just a dusting of down, curly locks, frilly, lacy and meaty earlobes, long, bony fingers, powerful wrists, hairy, naked chests, brawny arms and calves. Their character and level of education is of no interest but their body parts drive me wilder than truffles do a gourmet. What color are his eyes? *Colore di nocciola, colore di mare?*'

Whenever there was talk of men, it always brought out in Grandma a burst of one of Latin's daughter languages.

'No idea.' I was not inclined to explain the situation.

'Do take a look! When his eyes roll upwards in his death throes you can have a good look. Are his teeth beautiful?'

'Why should I care?'

'Well, isn't that crazy?' said Grandma with a laugh. 'Isn't that crazy? You really and truly want to have some tea? Coffee? I'll make some for you. The pipes are absolutely full of water. Tea leaves, coffee beans by the heap. And you want to go out in a snowstorm to have a drink. You should not move one millimetre.'

By this time I had put on my coat and shoes. I slammed the door and bounded down the stairs. I'd rather wait in the square, in the cold, than listen to any more of this. The conversation reminded of the time when against my better convictions I had introduced a school friend to Grandma, who had winked and licked her lips behind her back, indicating what a delicacy the kid would be. I'd wished the earth would swallow me up.

The snowflakes that fell from the deep purple sky, dirty with light, covered my horsehair winter coat. I relished the sight of the deserted streets so much that I skipped along, in so far as the weight of the coat allowed. I was there early, but I did not have to spend very long devouring the snow with my face turned towards the sky, because soon the figure of Jermák emerged from the flurries of snow.

## 15

'AM I BOTHERING YOU?'

'What's Norma-Elektra doing just now?'

'Elektra is working. She's translating a book about relationships.'

'What's it called?'

'*Adult Relationships*. We'll write the foreword to it together. But now I want to talk about you.'

I kept wondering when he was going to suck my blood. I suspected he intended to and I was genuinely curious as to how he would do it. Had I not felt uncomfortable with all the crowds around, I'd gladly have put my head in his lap so he wouldn't have to waste too much time. But, to put it somewhat crudely, I found him as repulsive as spinach purée.

'Your attitude seems a touch suspicious, Jerne, don't you think?'

'What attitude? I'm sitting here with you. Isn't that what you wanted?'

'I want nothing from you. I'd just like you to be present in my company in your natural state.'

'What for?'

'Now that's a hostile response, wouldn't you say? One of my principles is that the basis of a fruitful working relationship is the development, additionally, of a harmonious personal connection. What's your view of that?'

'It's not my intention to be hostile.'

'I know. But you're tense. Don't be tense! You needn't be afraid of me. Tell me, why are you afraid?'

'You said on the phone that you wanted to discuss my stories.'

'Of course I do. I'm very interested in your stories.'

'Really?'

'Contrary to Elektra's view I can see a future for your manuscript. Reading it I can sense that it has something striking. Just alter the emphases slightly and I think it's publishable.'

My inquiry as to what kind of revisions would have to be carried out triggered an avalanche of unimaginable proportions. From the first, introductory, section it emerged that I had before me a fanatical enthusiast of Propp and Bettelheim. Next, it became clear that the symbols would have to be ascribed significance. Moreover, it was only the symbols that had to be ascribed significance and the realistic trammels would have to be eliminated in order to fill the text with profound meaning. Thus

I'd be able to attract the attention of other forums and so break into the world of adult belles lettres.

'Seriously. It's by no means rare. I could give you countless examples of it happening.'

'I want to be a story writer.'

'A decent goal, but hardly very ambitious. Story writers are indeed read and loved, but real writers are respected, quoted and awarded prizes…'

'Your tea's getting cold.'

'So, rewrite the stories! Let the outline be so pared down that the deeper meaning immediately shows through. Believe me, I understand about these things. And if they're good, we'll publish. Somehow I get the feeling that we can work well together: I'll provide the sparks, you the realisation. I like surrounding myself with hard-working and reliable colleagues. As you know, I'm more of an ideas man.'

'Now I really have to go.'

I stood up and politely offered my hand.

'Thank you for the invitation.'

'And I thank you for coming,' said Jermák, and locked his hypnotic gaze into my feeble glance.

'I like you a lot,' he said. My eyes were caught for a moment. 'I like employees like you.'

I offered no reply to this, and made for the door, an idiotic grin frozen on my face. I did suspect that I was a good employee, but I didn't know I was quite that good.

# part v

## 16

ARRIVING HOME one Friday afternoon I popped into Grandma's room to say hello, only to find her packing furiously. She was standing on a stool, flinging her collection of horror books into a cardboard box, one at a time.

'I'm expecting a visitor.'

I pointed out that if it was her intention to create an unexceptionable, perhaps even distinctly friendly ambience, she might think, rather, about the black marble coffin standing in the corner, which served as her daytime place of repose. She paid not the slightest bit of attention to me. Even granted that guests always speculate about the character of their host on the basis of the titles on their bookshelves, I still couldn't understand why it was the books that had to be removed, rather than her other sanguinary requisites.

I settled down by the banana crate and began to poke around among the books. It was possibly quite a valuable collection; I'm really no expert. There were a number of first editions but the majority was what one might call trash. The original, 1897 edition of Bram Stoker's *Dracula*, read to shreds: Grandma always laughed herself silly at the idea that this single, not even very professional vampire aroused such unremitting horror. And about the end of the novel she would always remark that that was how 'some lousy band of ghostbusters' had taken her father out of action. So: it happens that thanks to my peculiar background I can read a classic horror story as documentation of my family history. Though I have to admit this kind of thing is hardly rare.

Naturally, there were other standard texts in the collection: Sheridan LeFanu's *Carmilla*, the collected poems of Coleridge, including 'Christabel', as well as Keats' 'La Belle Dame Sans Merci' in an anthology; Anne Rice's *Vampire Chronicles* – all of them character-forming staples of my childhood. But also strewn about were piles of vampire books in Latin, a publication in Gothic type about the horrific wolf-man of Bavaria (illustrated with woodcuts), as well as a number of scholarly treatises on Moldavian, Hungarian and Bohemian bloodsuckers. On the other hand it was really a shame to have wiped out forests of trees for the countless kilograms of books of terror and horror with scantily-clad, whip-wielding sluttish creatures on their covers. I could not explain the purchase of these in any other way except as the blind passion of the collector, otherwise it was unforgivable to defile with pornographic elements a living tradition so seriously grounded in scholarship.

'What kind of visitor?'

'A dinner guest.'

'Is it him who's having dinner or you?'

Grandma brushed my head with a thick collection of vampire jokes she had just taken off a shelf.

'That was very witty. Put it in!'

*Best Vampire Jokes*. New, expanded edition. I opened it somewhere in the middle.

'Grandma, do you know the one about the two vampires meeting…?'

'I know them all.'

We were silent for a few minutes, then I asked again:
'Who's coming?'
Grandma pursed her lips and gave me a piercing look.
'My husband.'
'I don't recall you having any kind of husband.'
'This is one of my older husbands.'

I was surprised. How old, I wondered? Because, for example when Grandma was fêted as a Rumanian baroness by London society in the 1890s, she had been engaged to an English aristocrat. I know Grandma's life story inside out and I'm rather fed up with it but, nonetheless, for me this episode is memorable because this was when she was introduced to Oscar Wilde, whom I have idolised and regarded as my model from the moment I understood the meaning of the English word indecency. At the time Grandma went by the name Lamia Constantinescu. A permanent bloodsucker. So: Miss Lamia was invited to a party, which was made all the more glamorous by the presence of Oscar Wilde. The hostess, Lady Everett, was much taken with Grandma's beauty and wanted to impress her by introducing her to the guest of honour. The professional wit and famed *bon vivant* was just letting a group of young men have the benefit of his pearls of wisdom as the two women approached him. From a distance of more than a century, Grandma recalls that Wilde was a repulsive man, though there was a mischievous glint in his eyes. Lady Everett introduced the young lady to the writer and then said:

'Mr Wilde, this flower in full bloom is happily engaged. In six weeks she will marry Lord Rupert Cleany.'

I don't actually remember the name Grandma said – Cleany happens to be the name of a brand of washing powder – but it suits him well, as he was said to be a clean-living, moral man. In any event, Oscar Wilde gave the exotic Rumanian beauty a pitying glance, adjusted his cufflinks to gain time, and then delivered himself of an aphorism: 'Marriage is the worthy end of a beautiful relationship, do you not think, young lady?'

Lady Everett gave a little frown but Miss Lamia laughed unbecomingly at the charming paradox. And until now I had thought – even if not as a result of this gem of wisdom but for rational reasons – that my grandmother had never married. Before the good lord could persuade her to come to the altar, she found a suitably Victorian excuse. She told him that she had not in fact been a sweet innocent girl for quite some time and this proved too much for Lord Rupert, just a little too much. So the gorgeous Baroness Lamia fled from the scandal to Vienna, where she subsequently chose her victims under the cognomen Elisabeth Bathori. The rest is history: ... *Wiener Blut, Wiener Blut.*

'But what kind of husband?'

'From the thirties.'

'He must be so old!'

'Never mind that, but how preternaturally young I am, considering we were the same age then.'

'Grandma, be a little enterprising! Tell him you are your granddaughter. But who is he? You've never told me about him. Who is he? What's his name?'

'Stop jabbering, Jerne. Pack your things, I don't want to see you here at the weekend. Would it be such an effort if just for a change you sucked someone's blood? I've got enough worries without you. My only husband is coming, your grandfather, whom I last saw on our wedding day.'

Though I felt that we had by no means exhausted the topic, Grandma had no intention of making me privy to any further details. Nor did I want to keep raising difficulties, fearing that an angry grandparent might actually do me harm. I conceded defeat and stuffed my rucksack with a change of underwear, some food and the three volumes of Marx's *Das Kapital*, which I had been meaning to read since the age of thirteen. I thought I could spend at least a night at the publisher's.

# 17

IT LOOKED as though Jermák had become a complete workaholic. He was still at his desk at 6.00 on a Friday evening and, as I entered, he turned energetically in my direction in his swivel chair.

'Well now, Jerne. Did you forget something here?' he said with a sardonic smile disguised as one of goodwill. 'Perhaps your heart?'

'What about you? Do you have so much on your plate?' I threw a question back at him grumpily. I was hoping he wouldn't let himself starve here until midnight, when he could set off to scavenge. Norma-Elektra was expecting him home, surely.

'Why should I hurry home? Elektra has gone away for the weekend to visit a girlfriend. But I'm glad to see I won't be alone.' He gave a short laugh and as his lips parted I could see a flash of his sharp canines.

'You guessed it. I forgot something. I'll see if I can find it and then I'll go.'

I hurried over to the smaller room and poked about in a perfunctory way. I took my purse out of my pocket to see if I had enough money for a hotel.

'Where are you off to with that huge rucksack?' Jermák had propped himself against the doorpost, blocking my exit.

'To my grandmother's.'

'Really? Your grandmother's still alive?'

'And how!'

'And you're a good granddaughter and are going to pay her a visit.'

'Yes.'

'She's one of those nice grannies, isn't she, who cooks delicious food and welcomes visitors with open arms? I'm so lonely this weekend. Couldn't I come with you to your grandmother's?'

'Unfortunately no. My grandmother can't cook and hates people. She can't abide anyone but me.'

'So, you're going to visit dear old granny. You are taking her a braided loaf and a bottle of wine.'

'Oh no I'm not. She's diabetic.'

Jermák's eyes narrowed and he licked his teeth. I was on the verge of crossing myself. If I had known how to.

'You staying and working?' I inquired with a feigned lack of interest, slinging my bag over one shoulder.

'I don't really know. Perhaps for another hour or so… I thought you'd stay a while longer… But there's no comfortable bed here… I don't like sleeping here.' He was having to force the words out slowly.

'Well, I'll be off then. Grandma's waiting.'

'Give her my best regards. I really wish her the best of health,' said Jermák and moved out of the way so I could pass with my rucksack.

'So I'll see you on Monday, then.'

'See you Monday, Jerne.'

It was my firm intention to wait until Jermák left the building and to steal back when he had done so. Not because I didn't have enough for a hotel. No, money was no problem. Rather, I was impelled by some kind of urge for adventure: what if I spent a few hours lurking behind a hoarding and then took the elevator up to the third? A Friday night out. So I hid behind a hoarding and watched the hurly-burly of the street. In fact almost no one came by, apart from a group of animal rights campaigners around 7.00, lugging shabby, moth-eaten furs and several nylon carrier bags full of gloss paint. They were probably heading for a furrier's downtown.

What's their problem, I thought as I eyed their comfortable leather shoes. In my opinion animals had a truly raw deal in the days when, of all the sexual perversions, bestiality still had pride of place. Neither cows nor stallions would have had a wink of sleep, so afraid would they have been of their masters. I'd hazard a guess that that's when the animals' hearts became so hardened that when one read the fables of the late Middle Ages and the early modern period they brought to mind Francis Bacon or the classics at the least provocation.

I spent the hours that remained meditating on the general welfare of animals. On the upper floor of the building the lights went out only around 10.00. A few minutes later I saw Jermák leave. I waited a little, in case he had to go back for anything, and then crept back into the building. As the lift creaked its way up, I found my keys. I listened for a moment by the door, then took the plunge and inserted the key into the lock. I felt my way along carefully in the dark, trying to find the light switch on the wall. Some light gathered around the mirror in the hallway, which reflected some of the lamps from the street. I patted my way along the wall but I couldn't find the switch.

I took a step back, in order to close the door which was still wide open behind me. Suddenly I felt hot breath on my neck. The cry stuck in my throat but as I tried to execute a 180-degree turn in order to confront the intruder, my right hand knocked against the mirror. It smashed to smithereens.

Jermák laughed mirthlessly, then his face suddenly clouded over and he stared at my hand. I followed his gaze. A fragment of the mirror had gashed open one of my fingers. Jermák grabbed hold of my wrist, lifted my hand to his mouth, and greedily, joyfully licked off the spilled blood. As the fine ridges of his tongue grazed my skin, my body twitched and shuddered as powerfully as one of Galvani's frogs. Despite this I was looking forward with interest to what would happen next. Jermák suddenly let go of my hand. He took a step back and bent down to gather up the splintered glass.

'So, it's you, is it?' he asked without looking up.

'My grandmother is not at home… And my sister has visitors… I wanted to spend the night here.'

I was almost telling the truth, but I couldn't have appeared all that self-assured.

'So you live with your sister? I didn't know that. And I…' He piled up the slivers on an old newspaper. '…I thought I'd collared an intruder. This is why I came back.' He picked up his wallet from the table. 'I only noticed it was missing when I was about to pay in the store.'

Our eyes met again as we both looked at my finger. I let it dangle and my ruby-red blood gathered under it, forming a little pool.

'Would you like a tissue?' Jermák asked without emotion. 'I'll tell Elektra it was I who broke the mirror, so she doesn't dock your wages.'

'I'm not bothered.'

'Wipe up the blood, will you? It'll look awful if it dries on the parquet flooring.'

'Of course.'

'I'll be off.'

'Bye.'

'Will you be in tomorrow?'

'No. I'm going to my grandmother's.'

'Like today?'

'Seriously.'

'Good night!'

'To you too.'

He left. I watched from the window as he disappeared down the deserted street. Then I went over to the basin and carefully washed from my finger the vampire's stinging saliva and the blood that had congealed on it. I walked round and round the room, sucking on the still-bleeding wound. I was in quite a state. I tried to weigh up my chances: life or death. After further careful deliberation, I concluded no greater calamity could now befall me, and a feeling of calm spread through my body.

# 18

ONLY A LONELY LEAF of curly parsley on a porcelain plate and an empty cup gave any hint that we'd had a visitor. This was perhaps only the third time in my life that I could recall such an event.

'Where's Grandpa?' I asked Grandma, who was gazing into the distance with the expression of a well-fed cobra on her face.

'Now that I have chopped him up and passed him through the electric meat grinder at maximum, he is no longer oppressed by the burden of being.'

'But Grandma! What's wrong? This isn't like you.'

It was only then that I noticed how lifeless her face was. I know I'm setting the bar high when I expect one of the living dead to be aglow with life, but I was stunned by how absolutely pale her face was even compared with its usual corpse-like pallor. She's family, after all.

'I'm exhausted. I've spent all night grinding meat.' Grandma stood up, gave the coffin a shove, and kicked the boxes filled with books under the bed. 'I don't feel like putting the room back the way it was.'

I made no move, in case she had a story to tell. I could see that she wanted to pour her heart out.

'You know, Jerne, when I first met him he was as handsome as young Ganymede himself, I drooled when I first caught sight of him. He was tall, lankily muscular, the skin on his face white as snow, his lips pink, his eyes so blue they made me dizzy. When he walked down the street, his hips swayed so that they drove you crazy, and the rays of the sun gilded his light-brown locks. He was the scion of a rich family, studying ancient history and oriental studies at the university. I was mad about him. I went to every rowing race, tennis party, first-night show, ball, lecture, wherever he made an appearance. I pursued him for a year and although my perfect looks had their effect, the final outcome was miserable: he asked for my hand in marriage. In the hope of becoming more intimate with him, I consented. Straight after our wedding he went off to the excavations at the sanctuary of Apollo at Delphi. I never saw him again. But he did leave me a lasting memento.'

Encouraged by how – unusually – Grandma had opened up, I asked gingerly:

'Boy or girl? I mean: the lasting memento.'

'And how the beauteous Narcissus had aged! Horror of horrors. To cap it all he wanted his wife to sign some document giving up her right of inheritance so he could designate a new beneficiary in his will. I said the person he was looking for had died long ago, that I was a granddaughter from her second marriage and didn't even know if my grandmother had been married before her marriage to my dear grandpapa. The object of my former desire had shrunk to a pitiful figure. He shuffled along with the aid of a stick, his false teeth clacked in his mouth as he ate, he was hard of hearing, he was senile, his hair was falling out, his body was wizened. Eternal life could have been his, had he only remained by my side! What a pair we made! The wedding guests were in raptures, everyone applauded the magnificent couple, never since the beginning of time had such a pair walked the earth. I still have the wedding photo somewhere, with my slim body nestling into his broad chest, a garland of myrtle in my freshly waved curls. He left me the following morning.'

'What a sad story.'

'Indeed. But the vile creature came back and is now in a good place. In the freezer. For the moment. I haven't decided what use to make of him later. But I have ideas.'

'I'd have liked to have met him, at least just the once.'

'What on earth for? He was an ugly old dog, sixty kilograms of bones, flesh, skin and guts. Take a look at this!' Grandma took a slime-covered gold ring from her pocket and carefully wiped it on the corner of her dark green, liana-patterned dressing gown. 'This wouldn't pass through the meat grinder. Jerne, did you ever study Latin?'

'No.'

'It's got some Latin text engraved on it. I think it's the family motto. Your grandfather came of noble stock, you know.'

'Like ninety per cent of the Hungarian populace.'

'He was a true aristocrat. One of the select few. Here, take it. It's yours.'

She dropped the ring in my lap. When I picked it up, I was surprised at how heavy it was. I read the engraved text: Anima muliebris virili corpore inclusa. I tried to put it on my finger but however much I liked the thought of a family ring, I threw the jewel back into Grandma's hand.

'You keep it. I don't wear rings and I shan't make an exception for this old-fashioned monstrosity.'

'Fine. I might just have it melted down.'

# 19

I FELT TIRED and it was difficult to keep up the pace at the weekend, so I collapsed on to my bed and didn't wake up until Sunday morning. Sunday mornings. At these times Grandma generally sat in her room with the curtains drawn, watching vampire films. She laughed a lot, having a great time, and liked me to sit with her so she could comment on the action, explain why Béla Lugosi was better than Boris Karloff, but usually I'm not inclined to do this.

'Him a vampire? In his dreams. Laughable.' Such were Grandma's desperate attempts to engage me in conversation. I resisted fiercely, in the room next door.

I sat cross-legged on the bed and reflected on why I always felt peaky on Sundays. I did feel rather nauseous, but considering that the entire Christian world was praying for the destruction of evil, I was in relatively good shape. After much hard thought, I came to the conclusion that the fresh air would do me good. I put on my coat, hat, scarf and gloves, and my hand was already on the doorknob when I suddenly heard Grandma give a growl. It was a very high-pitched growl, which may seem like a contradiction in terms, but isn't. I was curious. I went into her room. Without knocking.

'Well, what's up?' I asked.

'My pinkie has rotted away.'

'No!'

'Yes. I was channel-hopping, watching TV, there was a mass on one of the channels and for a few minutes I was lost amidst the church frescoes, the frenzy of the Baroque, but when I picked up the remote to change channels, my pinkie stayed in my lap. See?'

Indeed, there her little finger lay, now independent, in the palm of her hand.

'It's gone black so quickly!'

'Well, you know, at my age… You see, Hungary has once again become the land of Mary. What can we expect to come of it when Christmas comes and people will be spending three days together in loving harmony and longing for good?'

'Nothing good.'

Indeed, during the festival of love we forces of darkness are dogged by misfortune. We do have subterranean connections, no question: Grandma's notebook has Satan's phone number, too, but only to be on the safe side. I doubt that they talk very often.

'Well, my finger is not going to grow back. I have lost some of my charms.'

'Don't despair, Grandma. It's only a pinkie. Bye, Gran!' I waved goodbye. 'I'm going for a walk.'

I was already at the outside door when Grandma shouted after me.

'Jerne!'

'Yes?'

'Let's spend Christmas in Siberia! Remember how great it was last year?'

How great! We'd spent Christmas every blessed, or rather damned, year there since I was fourteen. Because the snow there is not the kind of icy, slushy holy water, like the snowstorm that once trapped her in Rome, with the Pope waving from his balcony. It ate its way through her fancy glad rags like hydrochloric acid, and every last piece had to be thrown out.

'In that case I'll order the plane tickets,' Grandma enthused.

'OK. Bye, Gran.' I was keen to be off.

'Wait!' Grandma burst out of her room. 'I'm coming with you. Let's see if we can find some godless hole in this city!'

# part VI

20

IT WAS NO DOUBT the severe loss of blood had taken its toll, for I normally found the Siberian winter pure joy: scooting along on a snowmobile, the company of the native peoples, etc. The winter lodgings where we had become regulars consisted of some ten houses standing in splendid isolation and was well-known as one of the hubs of tourism for Siberia scholars.

Nonetheless I quickly saw through Grandma's true intentions. Bitter though holy Christmas is, we could easily have spent our winter vacation in some more popular tourist paradise – but she wanted fresh reindeer blood. I recognized this as a legitimate desire on her part, for blood is life, blood is strength, but I was also quite clear that, while the thought did not make me lick my lips, locally this was a delicacy on a par with, say, deliciously-prepared dog in Korea. But in fact there's no need to go quite so far to find parallels, for Hungarian gastronomy offers a profusion of weird deviations. Meat jelly and tripe, those two good friends, for a start.

To cap it all, at first Grandma would not settle for anything but white reindeer, as that is truly special. This led me to a consideration of whether the difference between white and normal reindeer could be compared with that between Norwegian and Polish tinned liver of cod. My argument that the snow-colored delicacy is something even the locals happen upon only after an extensive hunt or by pure chance, and that its appearance would have to be a sign from heaven, something that in our present situation was not exactly to be desired, eventually calmed Grandma down, and she resigned herself to demanding merely young, plethoric wild reindeer.

From early morning on the second day of our stay she pestered me to stop sprawling on the log cabin's iron bedstead listening to the request programme on the eastern service of Radio Free Europe and instead go out and bag her a reindeer.

'But I don't even know Russian!' I protested.

'I really don't see why such a gap in your education should prevent you from shooting a wild animal.'

'Anyhow, you don't shoot reindeer,' I added, having just finished a highly informative book on reindeer hunting techniques. 'You lure it in.'

'First you lure it in, then you shoot it. I knew that.'

'What an act of cruelty that would be. I know better: first they lure the animal in carefully, then a rope is suddenly slung round its neck, then they batter it on the head until it collapses.'

'That is indeed much more humane. But it's something you could do yourself without a word of Russian.'

'Yes, Gran, but the Samoyeds use a rope sling to strangle reindeer.'

An hour later I was sulkily tramping chest-high in the snow, bundled up from chin to toe, six yards of rope in one hand and a substantial stick of wood in the other. What a sacrifice I was making! It was some satisfaction that Grandma was slogging along behind me with a local reindeer hunter while trying to brush up on the hundred or so words of conversational Russian she had picked up during the White Nights in St. Petersburg in 1912.

'Grandmama dear, did you know that in such freezing weather one's nose can freeze and simply drop off?' I called back to her mischievously, as it was still fresh in my memory how hard Grandma had found it to get over the loss of her pinkie. Only the other day I was still trying to explain how she could live a full and active life with just seven fingers, and now I was trying to make her feel as uncomfortable as I was in my borrowed, size forty, caterpillar-track snowshoes. At that moment I felt an agonising stab of pain: perfidy in my heart, boots one size too small on my feet.

'Some small fur-bearing creature,' Grandma said, communicating the words of the local deer hunter. 'I don't understand what he is saying, I'm just guessing from the way he keeps pointing to his fur hat.'

As Grandma bandaged up my foot, I tuned in to the Voice of America. I was barely conscious, so deeply had the animal trap gashed my leg. Dear oh dear, what will become of me?

'So do tell, what did they expect to trap in it?'

'Something furry, with a pelt that would not end up full of holes.'

That is to say, not me. No matter. For a few minutes, at least, I could imagine I was a fur-bearing animal.

# 21

WE ARRIVED BACK from Siberia in the first week of January and on the first day I was due back at work I didn't have the strength to even drag myself out of bed. I rang Norma-Elektra to say I was indisposed. I didn't tell Grandma I was awake, as I was not inclined to listen to her preaching another sermon about blood being the sap of life or any more arguments for the consumption of human blood. But she was suddenly there in my room without being summoned, leafing energetically through a Finnish cookery book in her hand.

'I'm trying to find a recipe for *crêpe sanglante*. I just saw one for rye bread made with reindeer blood.'

'Please don't mention reindeer blood.'

'I'm sure its nutritional value is incredibly high. It may be nothing more than a simple case of iron deficiency, which can be treated with a careful diet and appropriate medication. But I think this is something more serious, demanding a radical solution. What's your view of psychotherapy?'

'As a discipline or as a literary topic?'

'What I have in mind is finding a sympathetic specialist, who will give you a course of therapy to help overcome your inhibitions about sucking blood.'

'Who says I have inhibitions?'

'I know about such things. Analysis was all the rage in the thirties, I used to go myself.'

'You were in therapy?'

'In Buda, private practice, some Jew. In those days I had an officer, an army doctor, who kept saying: those damn Jews even make a profit from Christians' guilty feelings. Perhaps he was annoyed that while he was alive I made him pay for the sessions. He was a tall, willowy figure of a man, the psychiatrist I mean, that's why I went to him for so long, a couple of years. As for the officer, I sucked his blood for about a month. At first he didn't even notice, a hardened army man, as you may imagine. He kept saying that this is a country that has suffered a lot, and then suddenly his blood gave out.'

'And the psychiatrist? What kind of things did you tell him about yourself?'

'I told him everything in great detail: how I make my choice of men, how I seduce them, and how I sink my teeth into the flesh of their necks. You know, everything looks quite different in therapy. It's the job of the therapist not to be surprised by anything. They have special hands-on training about how to keep a completely straight face should a patient say "I have been sucking men's blood for two hundred years." He said I was a most interesting case, he even wrote it up in one of the specialist journals. So: we'll find you a specialist, you'll visit him for a while, tell him about your childhood, only broad-brush, mind, and you'll see how much better it will all be quite soon.'

'You think it will help?'

'Do you have a choice? And now I will make you some *crêpes sanglantes*. I'll just catch a few friendly fat rats from the stairwell…'

I must have looked panic-stricken, because Grandma added: 'You can't expect me to just grab a little kid from the playground! Not in broad daylight!'

# 22

I WOULD DESCRIBE in detail how I suffered if it didn't bore me to tears. I will just say that I felt unlocalisable physical pains from the top of my head to the tips of my toes. I was ravaged by a high fever and from time to time I spat blood – into a white bucket, just to demonstrate to Grandma how critical my condition was. What really put the lid on the whole business was a nausea that simply would not go away, to say nothing of my gaping wounds.

At first I thought I might lean out of the window and scan the population of the City Park with a spyglass, but then I had to admit that there was not a soul in the park, or indeed in the world, for whom I was prepared to get out of bed. So I just stared rigidly at the pages of a book and at selected spots on the walls, until night began to fall. Then I gathered all my strength and got up, so I could rest my elbows on the window ledge and watch Grandma let herself down the drainpipe of the block's rear courtyard. She kept swearing like a trooper, because in stilettos and a gold lamé cocktail dress it's quite difficult to clamber down metal piping, even if you can hang on to the withered tendrils of a Virginia creeper. But tradition is tradition.

An hour later I was thinking how an apathetic mood can easily make one prey to crazy ideas and that it would be better if I didn't stay at home and tried to find some way of passing the time. Just a couple of streets away were the licensed premises where Somi was performing with his band; somehow I managed to drag myself that far. I slammed open the door of the establishment, ordered half a pint of tomato juice, then rested my head on the bar. There was no music to be heard.

'Hiya, Jerke.'

'It's Jerne. Jerne.' Summoning what remained of my strength I managed to utter these words from my horizontal position, but I also had to open my eyes. Somi had a beer mug in his hand and stank nauseatingly of alcohol. I spat out a gob. I felt very ill.

'You're a charmer, Jeri.'

There would have been little point trying to be polite, I couldn't do it, I was just slithering around, my face a pale yellow.

'What's knocked you for six?'

'Perhaps I'm anaemic. I don't know.'

'Get yourself a Bloody Mary. Or,' said Somi, offering his white neck with a laugh, 'have a suck of my blood!'

For a couple of minutes I stared spellbound, like one of those celluloid vampires with plastic teeth, at his translucent veins. Something deep inside me began to stir, even though I hadn't seen that many vampire films. I ran my tongue over my lips.

'Shame you came by so late, Jerne, our gig was over half an hour ago. Then I quickly got so plastered that people can barely talk to me.'

'That gives me no pleasure at all.'

'You know, there was a time in my life when I didn't eat meat, never drank coffee, didn't smoke and didn't drink alcohol.'

'Eminently praiseworthy.'

'But the golden days of childhood must come to an end. Nowadays I don't deny myself anything.'

'This way you won't be very healthy when you die. You should take tranquilizers.'

'Becoming a star is taking its toll. We'll soon be cutting our first disc. We have a contract with a not very big but up-and-coming record company. We are up-and-coming, too.' He took a swig of his beer. 'We ought to change the name of the band. Of course Coitus Interruptus is bloody witty but the company wants something more mysterious. What do you think about Animal Triste?'

'Listen, Somi. Did you take Latin at school?'

'No, but I did pick up a thing or two at the Piarist High.'

We sat on the floor of the men's toilet, our backs against the tiles. A few minutes earlier Somi had sacrificed a joint on the altar of mutual pleasure. After a drag or two, he came out with it:

'How come you don't have anyone?'

'Do you have a woman or don't you?'

'It's a temporary state. Soon I will be a famous rock star and the screamers will be flinging their black lace knickers at me on the stage. Then after the concert I'll come from the dressing room and pick out three groupies writhing in ecstasy. Gather ye rosebuds while ye may. That's more than one rosebud, isn't it?'

'But why isn't there even one at the moment?'

'Because I'm building my career. That's what I'm focusing on. I don't have time for women.'

We fell silent. The sound of flushing could be heard from the cubicle next door.

He pushed his tongue into my mouth and his fingers between my legs. Of course, it could just as well have been vice versa. I was lost in wonderment. Why didn't I do this more often? I enjoyed the flash-like activity of the brain, especially those moments when it seemed that I didn't exist. But one of the flashes made me realize that my original goal was the sucking of blood. Suddenly, decisively, I sat bolt upright. Somi had taken off his shirt and his neck was available. Why. Why. Why. I threw myself across the bed. Somi's nimble fingers were hard at work on me.

'Would you ever have imagined when we were kneading wet sand in the playground that I'd be screwing you when we were grown up?' he panted, almost strangling himself with the effort of trying to rip off my clothes, because I just lay there like a sack of cement. 'Oh, if a UFO could see what I'm going to do to you!' Somi exulted and flipped me over on to my stomach.

At this point, however, my brain's flashing lights went out, even though in addition to sucking blood I did want to give sexual intercourse a try, because I had seen it written on a toilet wall that the best way to copulate was when you were high. I certainly wanted to find out if this kind of thing had a beneficial effect on migraine and a depressed frame of mind.

It was 3.00 in the morning when I again gave a sign of life and found myself virtually intact. Somi had also been knocked out; at some point he had given up on trying to undress me. There were certain indications that I was in my own room. I went out to the bathroom to quench my appalling thirst. I bumped into Grandma, who started to shout at the top of her voice that no granddaughter of hers was going to suck the blood of a drug fiend – who had ever heard of such a thing. I interjected that the smell penetrating the apartment was only marijuana.

'But he has it in his blood as well!'

We got into a hopeless argument about the harmful effects of mood-altering substances, which was only brought to an end by the first rays of the rising sun. Grandma then proposed that we divest ourselves of my guest. Immediately. We yanked the moth-eaten Persian carpet out of the wardrobe and rolled Somi's sleeping body up in it. With our combined efforts we managed to drag him down into the street and left him a few blocks down, in a doorway. It would have been the last straw if he'd woken up in our apartment. If he'd seen the framed picture of Vlad Țepeș, for instance.

'Won't he freeze?' I asked as we trudged home in the pink light of dawn.

'Nonsense!' said Grandma with a dismissive wave of her hand, but I could sense a fresh dose of disapproval welling up inside her.

'What's the matter?'

'Can you recall me ever – ever – bringing home any of my victims?' It was a blunt reproach. 'It's one of the ground rules, like you don't eat in bed.'

'But that's only so that the crumbs won't prick you.'

'In your case.'

# 23

HANS CHRISTIAN ANDERSEN was not liked by women. They laughed at him behind his back and were reluctant to dance with him. Even Jenny Lind, the Nightingale of the North, did not take him seriously as a man, though she valued him highly as a human being. But thankfully there's no need to be concerned, since the author of his most recent biography – to whom I hereby extend my greetings and grateful thanks for his conscientious labors – points out that the great storyteller masturbated regularly and also frequented brothels. This is good to know. I have a number of original observations regarding this, but one thing I am quite certain of is that the solidarity between women has been the ruin of many a man. They simply agreed amongst themselves that H. C. Andersen was a laughing stock and from that moment on, the fellow was out of the race, do what he would. Women. A filthy mafia, I tell you. Poor little Hans Christian. If he were alive this is what I would say to him:

'The world doesn't consist only of women. Don't give them the time of day, my friend!'

Women are dreadful. Once they have reached the age of thirty, they become convinced that someone on this planet has entrusted them with the maintenance of the social and other kinds of order. I had the feeling that this was the mania that had gripped Norma-Elektra. She had been fuming since morning, terrorising me as well as Jermák. I could hear clearly through two sets of closed doors how in the heat of a huge row she was bellowing at her husband that he and I were the two stumbling blocks to the rapid and successful achievement of the firm's work goals.

Personally I was of the opinion that Jermák alone was the stumbling block to the rapid and successful achievement of our work goals. When correcting what they had written or approved I found that while Norma-Elektra committed only the odd error in punctuation, Jermák – being a self-taught, cosmopolitan vampire – had absolutely no feel for syntax, for example. To say nothing of morphology or style.

Norma-Elektra's shrieking and howling continued, modulating into furious anger when Jermák poured a glass of water over her. A door slammed and one of them left. How excitable they both are, I thought. It was Jermák who had departed, because Norma-Elektra soon came in to keep an eye on me. On her pale blouse a palm-sized patch of damp was drying slowly.

'Jerne!'

'Yes?'

'I am in receipt of the third version of your stories. I will take a look at them.'

'Thank you.'

'Jerne! You don't do any of your story writing during working hours, do you?'

'I do sometimes think about them during my breaks at mid-morning, lunchtime and mid-afternoon.'

'Are you trying to be insulting?'

'By no means.'

'So you work all the time?'

'Naturally.'

'I still think that you concern yourself with other matters. When you visit the toilet you read literature in the bathroom. I have found periodicals in the bathtub!'

'Literary periodicals? I wasn't the one reading that stuff, you may be sure.'

'Well, who was then? Of the three of us you are the literature expert.'

'I don't allow myself to read literary periodicals.'

'Why not? Against your religion, is it?' Norma-Elektra looked at me as though I was an idiot.

'No. I'm scared that they might influence me. I don't want to be influenced by contemporary Hungarian literature.'

'Well then, watch out! If you're not careful you'll end up learning how to write decently,' Norma-Elektra declared, somewhat piqued, and moved away so that she could fume by herself.

I had lied. It was indeed I who had been reading those periodicals. But I'd tried to skim them quickly, so that they would have no influence on my art.

# part VII

## 24

THE FOLLOWING DAY Norma-Elektra had a number of errands to run, so I was continually glancing behind my back, wondering when and Co. would come and verbally harass me. Meanwhile I was working with my hands as fast as I could, as far as my morning-after condition permitted. Elektra was continually inventing things for me to do, to keep me in a state of perpetual motion. This time she had decided to target middle-schoolers with an anthology of verse. This is what I call an unbridled hunger for money but I could not indulge myself by voicing a countervailing view. I sat at my desk poker-faced, like a piece of machinery with a voice, checking the poems' punctuation.

There is in my soul not a single song; lyric for me is just the adjective from 'lyre'. Therefore, to keep up my spirits, I produced a list of the six most popular basic themes to be found in lyrical poetry, ranking them, as I went along, in order of frequency. These were the candidates:

1. You are beautiful and I love you
2. You don't love me

3. I don't love you
4. I am immortal
5. *Carpe diem*
6. The changes of the seasons

I patiently put a tick by each as I read the poems. Jermák looked in on me only towards lunchtime, when You are beautiful and I love you and *Carpe diem* – which from the very beginning had begun to draw away from the rest of the field – were fighting it out in the final round.

'What a pace you're setting!' Jermák noted. 'And I thought you were ill. Elektra told me you were indisposed. And you do look very pale.'

'You're nothing to write home about either.'

'Now, now, Jerne. There's that hostile tone again. I thought we had found some common ground…'

He leaned above me and whispered in my ear in a hoarse, strangulated voice:

'You taste good, Jerne…'

'Excuse me, but what is it that you want? I'm working.'

'To the question what it is that I want, I might answer: perhaps nothing.' He straightened up and took a few steps back. 'As to what I desire, I'd rather not say just now. When it has been fulfilled, I will share it with you,' he said, in a reverie. 'And you, Jerne, what is it that you want?'

Suddenly I remembered that in my days as a little vampire when I went to bed, if I couldn't get to sleep, Grandma would tell me a story. There was one that began like this:

*Far, far away, in the snow-capped mountains, in the times before the Trianon treaty, there stretched away into the sky on two stony outcrops two castles that faced each other. In each of them there lived a Count Dracula. They were constantly at fangs drawn, because their castles had been*

*built on either side of the same highway and they were*
*forced to share the travelers that happened to pass by, even*
*though these were few and far between, since the road was*
*full of potholes and led nowhere.*

'Why didn't they build a motorway?' I would suggest with child-like enthusiasm at this juncture, but Grandma would angrily bat this away: she was running late and I was still wide awake. Now, with the head of a twenty-something, I realize that the reason it was useful to listen to this story two hundred times was that I should be able to draw on it to solve the problems of my life.

'Let's spend a night together! From dusk until dawn,' I said, in reply to Jermák's question.

He was visibly shocked. He took a few steps back.

'Well, now. I'm having trouble breathing. Who would have imagined you harboured such thoughts in that head of yours.'

'Just focus on how we could make it a reality. We will be able to pit our strength against each other'– it was worth lifting entire turns of phrase from the story – 'and then see what we are made of.'

'I have no doubt about that. But I'm curious.'

He lingered a little by the doorway, scratching his chin.

'Have I frightened you?' I asked.

'By no means. I'm always glad if I've asked a good question. But for now I'll let you get on with your work,' said Jermák, and slunk out of the room.

*'Let's spend the night together, from dusk until dawn!'*
*said one of the vampires.*
*The other immediately rejoined:*
*'At least we will be able to pit our strength against*
*each other and then see what we are made of. To see which*
*one of us is the more cunning, the more wise, and the more*

*powerful. The winner shall have all the travelers that*
*happen to pass this way.'*
   *'So be it!' they roared in agreement and shook on it.*
*They agreed on a time and a place. Soon, the designated day*
*arrived and as night began to fall...*

In all likelihood one of the vampires won. I don't remember; I
could never be bothered to wait for the end of the story. It was
as boring as hell.

## 25

IN MY DREAM I was lying on an enormous, hard and uncomfortable
bed, set at the height of a lectern. Around me darkness enveloped
all, only my naked white body shone bright. A man's shape, also
unclad, emerged from the darkness. He clambered up on to the
bed, knelt on my stomach, held down my arms, and without
further ado bit into my neck. That's when I recognized my
assailant, Jermák. Like a passive sacrificial victim I tolerated
without resisting his extensive sucking of my blood, greedily
slurping and siphoning out of me all my strength. Then he began
systematically to tear off strips of my flesh, but I didn't protest
at this either. At last, he rolled off me. I lay in the blood-soaked
sheets, pieces of flesh all around me. Not a word passed between
us. Then I woke up.

   I lay there for a while and replayed the dream in my head so
that I would remember it later. I considered that both as regards
its theme and its action it was worthy of being shared with an
expert, should the therapy proposed by Grandma ever come to
pass.

   Drawing the curtain a little to one side, I peered out of the
window. It was sleeting, the scene painted in a thousand shades

*She was sad and embittered and in such a quandary that
one day she decided to seek out the wise old woman in her
village and ask her what on earth she could do.*

*'Never despair, my child,' the old witch consoled her, 'this
is something that is easy to remedy. Go home, bake three
shapely little pancakes and after dark go out into the woods.
Everything will be all right, you will see.'*

*And that's what the little girl did.*

So far, so good, but then came the active participation of the fox,
the wolf and the bear, in the course of which the story disabused
itself of every carefully-crafted metaphor. I tried to replace these
with practical implements, then I considered modifying the
gender of the protagonist – for example, making the little girl
into a little boy – because I thought that the situation that would
arise would offer countless possibilities. In the end I even made
a table of the functions that had to be fulfilled and the possible
substitutes, but I had to admit that my hands were seriously tied
by the fact that I would have had to put together that certain
something out of two bear paws, one wolf's snout and a fox's
tongue.

Suddenly someone put a hand on my shoulder. I didn't bother
to look up.

'You thought the office was empty?'

'Why? Were you here?'

'I've just come. But in future don't leave the door open! As
you can see, anyone could come in.'

'How did you find this place?'

'You mentioned the name of the street. And in this tiny street
there's only one publisher.'

'How strong the scent of your perfume is, Grandma. The
moment you were beside me, I knew it was you.'

'Indeed, something is needed to overcome the penetrating angel smell that's filled the apartment. It's like milk that's gone off.'

'I'm not surprised. There's an angel on my bed.'

'You don't say! Jerne, kindly get rid of him before I get home and give the apartment a thorough airing. And how did he get there, anyway?'

'How should I know? He came in through the window and that's it. Don't take it out on me!'

'Well, well! Perhaps the Christian God is what they say He is: selfless and everyone is equal in His sight. See: He orders a guardian angel even for those who are evil. What did he say?'

'Who?'

'The angel.'

'He doesn't speak. He is deaf and dumb.'

'Well, there you are. That's what they call employment for the disabled.'

'What have you come for?'

'I wanted to see what sort of people you are working with. But not a soul anywhere. Are they always this hard-working?'

'Yes, I don't know where they've got to. But it's none of my business. They are the bosses, I'm just an employee, I have to get on with my work.'

'Don't push yourself, my dear. A vampire was not made for labor. That was one of the reasons, among others, I made you study the arts. As a matter of fact, I've come to say goodbye. I've found a tempting last-minute offer and I'm off to Paris for the weekend. I'm ashamed to say I haven't been there since the time of the Jacobins.'

'That was not recently.'

'I was still alive then. Once I talked to Robespierre himself.'

'Well, well. And what did he have to say?'

'He said: "Cover your bosom, *citoyenne!*" and pressed his handkerchief into my hands.'

'You're lucky he didn't have your head chopped off!'

'They still knew how to make handkerchieves in those days…
And I was stupid enough not to keep it as a memento.'

'Have a good time in Paris!'

'Thanks. And deal with that angel! See you Sunday evening.'

Grandma picked up her pigskin suitcase and left.

Norma-Elektra burst in at 11.30, pushing a wheeled travel bag.

'Ah, Jerne, you're here? I told Ármin to give you a ring to say
we're not working today. I have to go off to a book fair and he's
already left for some conference.'

Ármin? I didn't know Jermák had another name.

'Of course, he forgot, just like he forgot to bring home this
catalog for me.' Norma-Elektra pulled out one of the booklets
from the pile on the table. 'Twice I told him. So I've had to come
and fetch it myself.'

'What shall I do about that final story?'

'Not now, my flight leaves in half an hour. We'll talk about it
next week.' From the doorway she called back:

'Go home! We're off today!'

I did indeed have to go home. The angel was slumbering
on my bed and still wearing nothing, so I was not surprised
he had covered himself with Grandma's 150-year-old crocheted
bedspread. He was breathing in and out steadily; saliva dripped
from the corner of his mouth, so peacefully was he sleeping. I
dialled a number.

'It's Jerne. Hello.'

'So you got my message.'

'Yes.'

'Good for you.'

'What now?'

'Meet you at the station, platform six, 5.00 a.m.'

'Right. I'll be there.'

'I'll be waiting for you.'

I put down the receiver. How conspiratorial! But no one can stop us. They are all on their way to warmer climes. I took down my rucksack from the top shelf of the wardrobe and packed a few necessities – penknife, candles, book of stories, diary, toothbrush and a change of underwear. I propped up the rucksack by the door and went into Grandma's room to choose some light reading to pass the time until dawn. I was looking for an action novel, but all I could find were boring romances. I opened one at random and found the following sentence: 'Now that I am truly happy…' And when the hero or heroine is happy in the middle of the story, it's certain he or she won't be by the end. This offered the prospect of a certain amount of interest, so I let myself sink into the book. It was a marzipan tale, with a bitter aftertaste. It was getting on for 3.30 by the time I finished. It was time to gather my things.

I was a little concerned that no one locked me in my room or forbade me from leaving the apartment. I was after all rushing headlong towards my ruin. I gave the angel a shake. He muttered something and rolled over. On the left side of his body the surface of his bare skin bore the delicate impression of the crocheted berry shapes of the bedspread. The vital thing, I thought as I laced up my walking boots, was to be on the alert every second. I will distract him, pounce, and then pretend nothing had happened. The winner is the one who is the first to knock the other off their perch of concentration. I waited a few more minutes, in case the angel woke, then slammed the door behind me.

## 27

BY THE TIME the sun rose, Jermák and I were trudging along a muddy track.

'Why are you called Jerne?'

'Why shouldn't I be?'

'Well, of course you can be. But how did you get this name?'
'I don't know.'

'And what's your sister's name? You live with your sister, don't you?'

'I do.' Oh dear. What is her name these days?

'So, what's her name?'

'You mean her maiden name?'

'She's married then?'

'No.'

'So?'

'She has a lot of stage names.'

'Is she in the theater?'

'No. To be frank, she uses them to fool the tax people.'

'All right, you don't want to give her name. But what do you call her?'

'Whatever name she happens to be using.'

'But what name did she get from your parents?'

'I don't know. That was before I was born.'

Jermák took a swing at a bush by the wayside with a large branch he had stripped of its leaves.

'Well, this name Jerne is a curious one at all events. I thought there might be a story behind it. There must be something that made your parents give you such an unusual name.'

'Why? Do you know why you are called Ármin?'

'Of course I do. My parents chose this name out of their profound respect for the work of the orientalist Ármin Vámbéry.'

'Ah.'

'Are your parents dead?'

'Why don't we change the subject?'

'Forgive me, I didn't want to upset you.'

'No problem. It's just a topic that doesn't interest me.'

We walked on in silence for a few minutes.

'So where are we going, actually?'

Jermák took a folded map from his back pocket.

'Here,' he said, pointing to a spot on the bank of the river.

'How much further to walk?'

'A mile or so.'

It was an average winter day: mist up to one's chest, ground frost, the bored crows on the trees constantly making a noise. The mist, a magical phenomenon. Many people favour fresh and clean air but I say that sometimes a mist is better. I was still a child when I was first fascinated by how, as it settled, it radically diminished visibility and relieved one of the necessity of confronting reality.

'Tell me something about yourself!' Jermák began again.

'What? Why don't you tell your story?'

'I'm willing to tell my story if you will tell me why you are curious about me.'

'For reasons of security.'

'Meaning?'

'I have to know what sort of person you are if I'm going to spend the night with you. According to everything I've read if we meet a stranger it is rather important to check whether the person concerned is not an evil incubus, because those are very active at night. But to be more realistic: I have to know whether you are not, for example, a perverted serial killer or a vampire.'

'There are no such things as vampires,' Jermák trilled. 'All the same, I'm absolutely delighted that I have managed to coax more than two short sentences out of you. Give me a kiss!'

'What? I wouldn't dream of it.'

'I just want us to be friends. For reasons of security. So that you won't stab me through the heart while I sleep.'

'You may rest assured about that.'

I moved over in front of him and embraced him. First I delicately bit into his lips, then I stuck my tongue in his mouth and for about a minute our saliva mingled. It was not especially hygienic but his trust in me increased straight away.

We trudged on. The crows made a fearful racket as they flew up from the branches of the poplars on our route.

'You're so different, Jerne,' said Jermák, as he casually kicked a dead baby crow out of the way. 'I've never met anyone like you.'

I looked at him suspiciously.

'Why do you say that?'

'Because that's how I feel.'

'I see,' I nodded. 'How much further?'

'Nearly there.'

Indeed, the hut could now be seen by the riverbank.

'I can hardly wait, I'm so curious about our night together.'

'Another few hundred yards, and you'll find out,' I assured him.

'You have me in your spell with your desire.'

'I hope you will also have me in yours.'

'I've no doubts about that. You know what I have in mind…'

'Yes, yes, but now let's hurry. I'm getting cold.'

There was still plenty of time to collect some kindling before dusk. We found some dry twigs and a few thicker branches that were lying around. All the equipment we found in the shed was old and rusty, but we managed to chop up enough wood to keep us warm for the night. The helve of the axe damaged the skin on our palms. As I entered the hut, I kicked off my boots and settled down by the tiny stove. It needed time to heat up.

'Well, I'll just read today's paper,' I said and laid it out before me.

## 28

GRANDMA RETURNED on Sunday night. Her first words to me were:

'Imagine, someone called me a Jew on the underground.'

'Why didn't you take a taxi?'

'I only had euros on me, I thought I could risk taking the underground without a ticket. And then this thing comes up to me and says "Hey, you Jewish women are not that bad looking".'

'But that's a compliment.'

'And how! I'd have liked to tell him, hey, you blind crow, this is a vampire nose, not a Jewish nose. And then at his throat, no messing.'

'Grandma, I'm too tired just now to discuss Jew-calling, Christian-calling, or vampire-calling,' I groaned and collapsed on to the nearest chair.

'Are you indeed? And why are you so tired?'

'Grandma,' and I paused for effect. 'I sucked blood last night.'

'Really? That's wonderful. Man, woman or child?'

'Does it matter?... Man.'

'Hmm. A good start. Promising. How did it happen? Who is the lucky victim? Out with it!'

'That's my secret.'

'The important thing is that you've done it at last. It would be in bad taste to grill you, if you're not going to tell the story yourself.'

Grandma checked her nose in the mirror and didn't even glance at me. 'Though I always tell you every detail. Undoubtedly...' She covered part of her nose and now looked at it in the mirror at various angles. '...this fills me with confidence regarding your future. You have no idea how relieved I am. But what about the psychotherapist?'

'What psychotherapist?'

'The one I've arranged an appointment with. Your eating disorder, you know.'

'Visit him yourself!'

'Me? I'm happy and well-balanced.'

'If you tell him about just one of your days, you'll be sectioned along with your crazy ideas.'

'Hey! Don't you try and make me think I'm ill! In my case it's not a question of imagining I'm a vampire, I really am a vampire. A vampire entirely at peace with her fate and fully functional. This is a possibility open to you as well. But now tell me, Jerne, is this a vampire nose or a Jewish nose?'

'What does it matter, so long as it's gorgeous?'

# part VIII

## 29

'THIS STORY is so obscene that there is no question we have to leave it out,' said Norma-Elektra laying down the law about the story of the little girl who was lacking something. We were in the middle of our usual Monday morning business meeting.

'But what shall we put in its place?'

'A similar story with something lacking. What would you say to "What the man takes away on horseback, the woman brings back in her apron?"' I interposed.

'That's the other way round, Jerne,' said Elektra correcting me. '"What the man brings home on horseback, the woman carries away in her apron." I think the story is rather sexist, don't you?'

'I do, I do,' I nodded in agreement.

'Let's find something else! Something with an animal in it. Any suggestions, Ármin?'

Jermák had taken no part in the discussion so far and was just fiddling about with his ballpoint.

'I don't know. I haven't thought about it yet.'

'Well, think about it now. You have equal responsibility for every publication, not just me. Even if it's just a book of stories.'

'Elektra, my dear, I think we can safely leave this in Jerne's hands. She knows all there is to know about stories.'

'I have no reason to question Jerne's expertise, but the book will still carry the imprint Elektra and Co.'

'Fine, fine. Then let's have the one where the owl takes everyone for a ride.'

'You're right, my dear. "The Clever Owl" is a wonderful, symbolic tale. Go over the text, Jerne, and we're done. I must be off, I have to be at the printer's by 10.00. Ármin, will you come with me?'

'Not now. I'm not ready with the preface yet.'

'But I have to bring the books over.'

'You're a strong woman.'

'I'll gladly come with you, Elektra,' I offered.

'No, Jerne, you just stay and do the owl. I'll go by myself.'

I hurried off into the office without a backward glance. Soon the door slammed and Norma-Elektra had left the scene. Jermák waited, out of tactical considerations.

'How are you?' I inquired politely, with barely disguised horror on my face when, half an hour later, he finally decided to seek out my desk.

'I'm quite well, though a little tired. But if the reason for my exhaustion is the night spent with you, I always want to be this weak.'

'I can't imagine what exhausted you.'

'I believe it was the detailed scrutiny of the financial pages that sapped all my strength.'

'Sorry to hear that.'

'No problem,' said Jermák calmly and placed his hands on my shoulders.

'I fear you have certain thoughts lurking in the back of your mind. Nothing happened.'

'I don't have any thoughts lurking. Lurking? Thoughts?'

'In that case, let's get back to work.'

'Wait a moment! Let's sit down.'

'I'm already sitting down.'

He sat down too.

'Jerne, there's nothing I can take away from you. I have all I need. None the less, what lies behind your defenses attracts me. I have no wish to win you over, I don't want to compete with you…'

I frowned. There are few things more vexing than to discover that someone you presumed was a vampire turns out to be little more than a cheap romantic hero.

'…I want to be with you just the way you are.'

'Ah,' came my scintillating response.

Jermák let out a hysterical howl of laughter.

'So that's it? That's all you can see? Is it all that simple?'

'What is it that I am supposed to notice?'

'My heart is pounding. Your voice sounds more subdued. The sun has moved away from behind my head…'

'Why? Is that where it has been until now?'

'I have to tell Elektra.'

'Tell her what?'

'It's essential to clear the air.'

'Why?'

'It's a matter of honor.'

'I don't insist.'

'Because it's dawned on me that it's you that I want. What about you?'

'It hasn't dawned on me yet.'

'It will.' Jermák jumped up from his chair and patted me on the back. 'No hurry. I'll give you time to think. Accept your thoughts, even if you don't agree with them. We'll talk later.'

# 30

WHAT DID BEGIN to dawn on me was the conviction that I had somehow messed things up when sucking blood. I considered asking Grandma for advice on what to do in such circumstances. I was making my way home through the park when it suddenly occurred to me that the squirrel could well be something that half the village possessed and only a little girl lacked. With its coat of russet fur, it was a nimble little creature that readily scrambled up and down tree trunks. But it did not really add up. A squirrel has paws, a tail, a tongue but still, that didn't add up. It was an intractable, unresolvable story with a lack. If I had to categorize it, it would be a VIII.a.2, but perhaps even an a.3.

I was walking along the same track as I always did in the summer, but now I sank ankle-deep in the dirty slush. In the twilight I couldn't see that the snow had melted quite so much and that the night frost had not yet set in. I was a shivering wreck by the time I reached our front door. I sloshed my way up to the fifth floor and while still on the stairs I was thinking about that wonderfully numbing sensation you get when you sink neck-deep into a warm bath. I began to strip off in the hallway, flinging my hat and scarf on the floor, kicking off my soggy, squeaky footwear, and pushed the bathroom door in as I unbuttoned my coat, ready to turn on the tap. And then I had a surprise.

'Grandma, what is this?' I shouted at the top of my voice, as I was overcome by fury.

No reply.

'For crying out loud, Grandma, I know you're home,' I swore.

Nothing stirred. I rolled my sodden socks off my feet and continued to yell:

'Grandma! Grandma! I know you can hear me even in the coffin.'

I flipped the lid open. And indeed there she was, eyes tightly closed. I bawled in her ear.

'What is that in the bathtub?'

'My dear, why don't you let me rest? I'm going to have a tiring night. Is it my bloodbath that's upsetting you?'

'So, it's a bloodbath.'

'Take a dip yourself! You'll see, it'll do you good. It rejuvenates.'

'Hot water would do me. I got chilled to the bone on the way home.'

'It'll warm you up, too.'

'You're not seriously suggesting I get into a bathful of blood?'

'Why not? It did the trick for Elisabeth Bathori.'

'That was a show trial, Grandma, did no one tell you? I'm going to drain the bath if you won't.'

'You'll do no such thing. It took all the blood from my pets to get that. I put in some anti-coagulant, too, so I can take a bath tomorrow as well. Don't you dare touch it!'

'Or else?'

'Or else your granny will put her sweet little grandchild through the meat grinder.'

'Thanks. That's charming.'

'Life is cruel, my dear. Dog eat dog. This applies even more to vampires.'

I slammed down the coffin lid. I gritted my teeth, but then family life is not always a bowl of cherries.

# 31

'MAY I COME IN?'

The day at work had so far passed very peacefully. In the morning Norma-Elektra had inquired cheerfully where I had picked up my sensuous, nasal tone of voice and from this I deduced that she had no idea how, behind her back, I was undermining her happy relationship with her husband by my sheer existence. I went on tenaciously extirpating spelling errors until 4.00 in the afternoon, and had plenty of time to reflect. What was mainly concerning me is what I would do in the event that Norma-Elektra decided to take on my manuscript and offered me money for it. It seemed unacceptable to me to make a profit from an institution like Elektra and Co. Publishers, an institution that fulfilled the noblest of goals. If Elektra were determined to foist a sum of money on me, I would reply:

'No, I cannot accept it. I did this out of sheer enjoyment, it would please me more if I could pay you for allowing me to do it. It is impossible to put a price on letting the spirit soar twenty-four hours a day.'

If she insisted and there was nothing else for it, I would accept the wad of notes and offer them to some suitable foundation of my choice. Grandma had piles of money; why should I bleed a publisher dry?

Story writing or bust. I could see that I ought not to be so passionately devoted to a cover activity, bearing in mind, too, that my terrestrial mission was not this but rather the sucking of humankind's blood. I ought in any event strive to achieve some kind of healthy balance, I decided, but when I got to this point, my thoughts wandered unbidden in the direction of carrot cake.

In one of the scenes in the story cycle I was writing, carrot cake is very much at the heart of the action. What if, adopting a child-centric attitude, I were to attach as an appendix a recipe for carrot cake, in case the children reading the story were impelled to knock up a little dessert? It would be a charming gesture and, if I remembered correctly, it was just gestures such as these that Norma-Elektra had found wanting hitherto. I went off to the storeroom to research the topic. I did indeed find cookery books, but it was obvious that for the organic cuisine movement even carrot cake was too decadent a concept.

'May I come in?' asked Jermák, but he was already inside the room.

All the reading had made me dizzy, so I had sat down and propped my head against the wall.

'Norma-Elektra?' I inquired, genuine curiosity in my voice.

'She's gone home. We're on our own.'

'Excellent.'

'Isn't it?'

'You did detect the irony in my tone, I hope?'

'I don't believe you. You're glad.'

'Of course I'm not glad.'

'Perhaps you'd prefer it if I just walked past you in the future, without turning my head? Jerne! Our time has come!'

'Our time? No such thing. Perhaps in another life.'

Twenty-five hardbound volumes of lesser catechisms were pressing against my side.

'If you can see the true path, why don't you take it?'

'Is there more than one path?'

'You like playing games, don't you? Count me in. Just tell me in advance what it is that we're playing.'

Jermák began to circle the piles of books cautiously, heading in my direction. I sat in the corner, cookery books in my lap.

'Stay where you are, I'm coming,' he assured me.

I did not stir. I waited for him to come. With a final bound he tried to clear the heap consisting of some still-unsold dream-books, but he couldn't lift his left leg high enough and, losing his balance, he came crashing down on me with the full weight of his body. As his skin touched mine, I lost all my self-control. I wanted to slurp his blood again, that delicious, hot, fat-rich blood that I had already once tasted. I did not hesitate a second and began to tear his shirt off to liberate his neck as soon as I could.

'I know you wanted this too,' he panted into my ear.

I tried to find the most suitable site on his neck.

'Have you found that wretched book yet?' came Norma-Elektra's call from the doorway.

I quickly withdrew my teeth from Jermák's neck and tried to push his body off mine. Norma-Elektra stared at this unlikely coupling with eyes like saucers.

'Well, this is how it is,' Jermák mumbled as he clambered off me.

He slowly struggled to his feet and, knocking over several piles of books in the process, set off after Norma-Elektra, as his co-owner had turned and run away, slamming the storeroom door behind her.

I tried to regain my composure. As I straightened up, the buttons of Jermák's shirt in my lap scattered in every direction. Looking down on the floor to count them, I spotted a booklet entitled *100 Dishes With Carrots* in a far corner. So – the afternoon had not been entirely wasted after all. I picked up the collection of recipes and strolled out of the building. I didn't lock up, thinking the owners would soon have had enough of chasing each other around and return to their premises.

It did concern me, however, what happens to vampires when they are discovered practising their dark arts. I mean: before they are stabbed through the heart. I was also preoccupied by the following thought: at what angle had Norma-Elektra seen me as I was busying myself with her partner's neck. I tried to reassure myself that perhaps from a certain distance the spectacle offered quite a different perspective and that therefore I might get away with being no more than a co-respondent in an adultery case. Fortunately the official view is that there are no such things as witches, vampires, wolf-men or ghosts, and therefore I would escape a lonely death on a pyre well before the universal mass orgy that the Christians have been promoting under the name of the Last Judgement, when we evil folk will be destroyed to the last man and woman.

Grandma was racked by a migraine. The angel was kneeling before the sofa, massaging her temples. I watched them from the doorway.

'A little higher. There, there. That feels so good, please don't stop.' I set off for my room.

Grandma shouted after me.

'There was a man asking for you on the phone, but I can't remember what he wanted.'

'Thanks, Grandma.'

'Was it anything important?'

'I'm sure it wasn't.'

'What delicate little hands this sweet angel has.'

'Forgive me, Grandma, I'd like to make a phone call.' I closed the door, so the ecstatic little groans would not be audible over the phone.

I dialled.

'Hello, Elektra. It's Jerne.'

'Hello.'

'I think that storeroom business could be misconstrued.'

'I don't think it could. I think it was pretty straightforward. You were wasting company time.'

What a relief.

'Unfortunately. But not in the way you imagine.'

'In what way then?'

'I'd like to have a word with you.'

'You want to offer some kind of excuse?'

'To have a word.'

'A word. Oh, all right. A word, then.'

# part IX

## 32

NORMA-ELEKTRA was waiting for me. I gave her a gracious smile, but her eyes were ablaze and it was immediately clear that this would not be enough. I got down to business straight away; there was no point discussing the vagaries of the weather.

'I'm completely innocent.' As it happened, this wasn't true, I was merely being rhetorical. 'I'd like you to know that I am on your side.'

'I wouldn't like you to think that I don't set some store by your empathy and solidarity, but these are hardly enough. Can you explain to me how you came to be in such an intimate bodily configuration, if it is nothing to do with you? If I saw aright, you were just about to...'

'Kiss his neck.'

'I see. I thought you were biting him. No matter. Both presuppose a bodily proximity that goes beyond the notion of a harmonious working relationship.'

'How did he put it?'

'He confessed everything.'

'Everything?'

'You know, there are men who torture their partners with honest confessions. The only reason they talk of decency is so that they can see the other suffer and exercise their own power. That is what they have in lieu of a conscience.'

In all probability Norma-Elektra believed that her life partner was a somewhat shifty, spineless and deceitful creature. But I decided I would not enlighten her that she was in fact sharing her bed with a dysfunctional vampire.

'He has no secrets from me. He told me everything, down to the smallest detail. The whole story, exactly as it happened.'

Well, now. Hardly.

'I know he sometimes has moments of weakness. His self-control does, on occasion, leave something to be desired.' It was obvious Norma-Elektra was intent on making a longer speech. 'But we have lived together too long for this to matter. You couldn't imagine all that we have been through together. Our relationship is based on mutual respect and that is why it is so resilient even amidst the gravest of difficulties.'

I suspected we were only just now amidst.

'There are times he strays off the straight and narrow, but our bond remains intact and we support each other in a spiritual partnership that is beyond any rapacious desire of the flesh. After every trough of the wave we launch ourselves on the sea of life with renewed vigor and strength. We will work better together from now on than we ever did before, you know, Jerne.'

I was astounded. What a neat little speech. I almost forgot why I had come, until the last sentence jolted me into a realisation:

'I'm sacked, right?'

'Nonsense. Don't say such silly things. You are not "sacked", I'm simply suspending you from your position with immediate effect and will find someone else to carry out your duties. Don't come here again. And I need hardly say that after all this I am not in the least inclined to squander my money on publishing your dilettante efforts in book form. Try another publisher, perhaps.

At all events, I'm glad I've managed to limit my losses. But I'm genuinely surprised that you, of all people…'

'Why?'

'You know very well.'

'Oh, that? I'm sorry things have turned out like this.'

'Don't be. Just don't come anywhere near us ever again.'


# 33

SO I SET OFF HOME. For some obscure reason I felt that life was smiling at me. Perhaps it was that little chemical manipulation in the morning, or the glittering snow crunching underfoot in the several degrees of frost, or the sunshine and the clean, fresh air that created this illusion. By way of compensation for the little *malheur* yesterday I bought myself some fresh blood oranges at a grocer's and crossed the park dangling them in their bag. Oh, how light was my soul!

On the road leading out of the park stood a white minibus surrounded by a group of five or six figures. I recognized Somi, and he me, because he waved and ran towards me. I had not heard from him since we had rolled him in front of number sixty-three.

'Hiya. You on your way home?'

'Yes.'

'There's something I'd like to ask you.'

'Fire away.'

'I'd like to know,' Somi said scratching his back, 'what happened to me that night, because in the morning I found myself lying next to a wheelie bin overflowing with rubbish, and that can't have been my destination.'

'Oh, I wouldn't be so sure.'

'Please, don't try to be so witty. It's a serious question.'

'How much do you remember?'

'You were sprawled across the bar, you felt sick, you were coughing up blood. Then I took out a spliff…'

'Which we smoked.'

'Yes, in the men's toilet. And then?'

'Then nothing. We went home.'

'Separately?'

'Yes.'

'Strange. I seem to recall it otherwise.'

'For example?'

'Or did I just imagine it?'

'What?'

'You say we didn't do anything?'

'What would we have done?'

'For example, I'd like to know if we screwed. Because I seem to recall that we were about to.'

'Come now.'

'Because if we did, screw I mean, then I thought maybe you're expecting us to screw again. But then I couldn't just give you a buzz and say "Hey, Jerne, did we fuck last night?" could I?'

'No, indeed not.'

'I'm so glad we ran into each other. 'Cos it's pretty shitty to just ask if we screwed or not. I don't even remember whether it was good. And then what if it was? It's one big fog, and you're expecting me to come again. That's what was worrying me.'

'It needn't have done.'

'Anyhow, what's up? Are you OK?'

'Yes.'

'We're just off. We're playing out in the sticks tonight.'

'Still Coitus Interruptus?'

'Spare me. For all I care it could be Fellatio, but we just can't agree on anything. Everyone's pulling in different directions. But things are going well on the whole. I'll soon be a rock star, you'll see. But are you really all right? What's up with that rabbit, eh?'

'It's raiding patisseries.'

'That's good. Carrot cake, eh? That's what turns rabbits on.'

'Of course.'

'Listen, Jerne. Are you sure we didn't? Sure we didn't screw?'

'We didn't.'

'I'm sure I'd like to fuck you, that's why I'm having such dreams. No matter. What are you doing tomorrow?'

'Why, what do you have in mind?'

'You know, that's what I really like about you, the way you talk to everyone as if you wanted to puke on them. It's so punk.'

'Thanks.'

'It would be great to meet and we could then go for a beer or something…'

'I think they are waving to you from the bus.'

'Must be off. We'll take it from here next time.'

He waved goodbye and I watched as he ran back to the minibus. I was moved.

# 34

I RANG THE BELL three times because I didn't feel like fishing out my key. Soon the angel peeped out of the spyhole but didn't open up. I had to dig around in my rucksack after all. I entered full of cheer, aglow with life but somehow the reception was crappy. I took off my coat and just revelled in the central heating for a minute or two. The angel was leaning against the wall in the hallway and giving me looks that could kill. Pinned to the mirror was a brief message from Grandma: *The psychiatrist. Back in the morning perhaps.* He must be a fairly juicy piece for Grandma to devote so much time to him. Well, that's one guy that won't be treating me, I told myself.

All of a sudden the angel came up to me ostentatiously and kicked me forcefully on the ankle. I gave a hiss of pain.

'Now that's no way to settle things, friend,' I said with as much deliberation and loftinesss as a trainee vampire could muster.

The angel stood facing me with arms provocatively akimbo. He stared straight at me.

'Well, what is it, my angel?' I said pompously.

The angel retained his confrontational pose and remained silent. From the mussed up reading matter I concluded that he was no stranger to the written word. I gave him my fountain pen and a piece of paper I found on the table.

'Write it down.'

'I know everything.' Wonderful. Everyone knows everything. And so?

'And how come you know everything?'

Instead of appealing to supernatural forces the angel pointed to my leather-bound diary, where I wrote up the sweet secrets of my life every night.

'That's very cunning of you,' I said, admitting the angel's resourcefulness.

'You have sinned,' he scrawled with great difficulty.

I thought for a moment. But nothing came to mind.

'Your sin is rank, nothing can wash it off.'

'Well now, which one?'

He was taken aback for a moment. He pondered a while, then wrote: 'All of them.' I was beginning to lose my temper. What was he doing bandying such accusations around?

'I have no sins. Full stop.'

'You are damned.' These were the next words of my winged friend.

'Now, you listen to me. I did not ask you to come here. If I don't reproach you for getting into my bed, messing up my books, reading my diary, and hanging round all day stark naked, don't *you* dare tell me off! You hear me? Get out of here! Go and Marquis de Sade off!' I roared, beside myself with rage.

The last time I had been so angry was when I found the news stand had sold out of all the literary periodicals. The angel tore up the piece of paper and smashed his fist into my face. He sat down on the bed. I went out into the kitchen for some ice.

# 35

AS SHE SAID she might, Grandma did come home in the early morning. I told her I had lost my job and that I'd like to go back to England. She opined that it was not a good idea for a beginner to try to launch her career there, as England was a bastion of Anglo-Saxon vampirism, and in any case those who come from the provinces had no chance of a look-in. She suggested that I become a writer full-time, until I die. Of course, I could continue to write after becoming a vampire, too; it would come in handy as a cover. She promised to get my stories published privately, as she had recently made a largish sum on some clever deal and had a bit to splash around.

I had of course made peace with the angel by 9.00 the following morning. I hadn't the heart to be really angry with him, he seemed to be such an innocent and placid creature. He'd let his fist get the better of him, but then these things happen. Compared with his unequivocally aggressive and militant behaviour on Wednesday afternoon he had retreated into himself and was sitting on the bed reading. A veritable little bookworm. He'd read every single one of my books and, to keep him occupied, I'd had to bring vampire novels from Grandma's collection to ensure a steady supply of quality reading matter. It didn't look as though he was thinking of leaving. Grandma didn't mind, saying that our guest was a blessing, for he was able to do many things with great skill.

Some time around 7.00, someone rang the doorbell with particular aggression. I only opened the door a crack, leaving it on the chain. Somi poked his blonde head round the door.

'Hiya. Thought I'd come and see your stamp collection,' he said, adjusting the cobalt-blue silk cravat around his neck.

'How did you find us?'

'By having been here before. You're not going to deny that to my face, are you? Can I come in?'

I opened the door wide. By the time I caught up with him, Somi was admiring the angel's genitalia.

'Now, I'm no slouch in that department, but I have to say that's really rather respectable. Not disturbing you, Jerne, am I? *Post coitum*, maybe?'

'Would you like some tea?' I responded.

'Don't you have anything a bit more macho?'

'No.'

'Then tea it is.'

I went off to the kitchen, Somi hard on my heels. This did not make me happy, as our kitchen is not fit for human eyes. And not just because Grandma occasionally uses it as an abattoir but, rather, because we don't do any washing up. The dirty dishes we simply throw out. Kitchen waste stood rotting in several sacks under the window. Grandma hadn't even rinsed out the meat grinder after Grandpa.

'Hey, Jerne, won't you ask the guy if he wants any tea?' Somi asked as I tried to dig out the kettle from under a pile of vegetable debris. Last week it had got so filthy, I almost threw it out.

'He's dumb. And he only eats manna,' I replied.

'It's not serious then.'

'What?'

'With this guy.'

'No. We just live in the same room and sleep in the same bed.'

'And does he have to be here?'

'He won't leave.'

'Peculiar set-up,' Somi muttered and buried his face in his hands. He blew his nose. 'This makes things a bit complicated, Jerne. Are you listening to me?'

'I am.'

'Yesterday, as we were coming home from the gig in the small hours and I stared out of the bus window into the dark night, I realized a whole bunch of things. For instance, that since the time we almost screwed, I can't get you out of my head. I'd wanted to fuck you before, but now I do even more. You're the first thing I think of when I wake, and the last before I fall asleep. I don't know how you've felt about this since...'

'But we didn't even...'

'Yes, I know, but don't try to pretend we didn't roll around in the bed where the naked guy is now reading. You were mean yesterday and tried to deny it, but you do remember, Jerne, don't you? True?'

'True.'

'So. I've come because I don't want the girls screaming any more when I take off my tee shirt.' To add weight to his words he stood up and began to unbutton his pink shirt. 'What I want is for *you* to admire my torso.'

The sound of the telephone interrupted this sincere declaration.

'Jerne, it's for you!' came Grandma's voice from the other room.

While I was on the phone, Somi built a little igloo out of sugar cubes. He had unbuttoned his distinctly dandyish item of clothing and laid it on the radiator to avoid it getting creased. I was so moved I could barely speak.

'Forgive me,' I said, excusing myself. 'I can't offer you tea just now. I have to go at once. I'll call you tomorrow, OK?'

## 36

MY RENDEZVOUS was in the City Park, in front of a castle built in the eclectic style. It had been constructed for the millennial celebrations as a pavilion originally designed to represent various Hungarian styles and was rebuilt in more durable materials because it had been such a success. But sensation-seeking guides had no qualms about suggesting to their largely Anglo-Saxon tourist groups that it was an exact copy of Dracula's castle. And they happily swallowed this claim hook, line and sinker, and indeed passed on the suggestion to all and sundry.

I waited in the dry bed of the artificial lake. These Hungarians are pretty filthy, with all their litter, I decided, and set off for a bench that had been deprived of several of its wooden slats. I heard a noise, the sound of panting, but before I could turn around two hands grasped me by the shoulders.

'Is this how you always come,' I said, 'attacking me from the rear?'

'I saw you from the crossroads and ran to catch up with you,' wheezed Jermák. 'Come on, let's sit down over there, on the bench.'

'Why did you summon me here?'

'Why did you come?'

'Only for my pyjamas. You said on the phone I'd left my pyjamas.'

'Here you are.' Jermák handed me an A4-size cardboard wrapper. 'I absent-mindedly stuffed it in my own rucksack.'

'Lucky that Norma-Elektra didn't find it. Well then… Ciao.'

'Wait… Aren't you even going to say goodbye? I heard from Elektra you're no longer working for us.'

'Are you surprised?'

'I'll miss you. But this is how it has to be.'

'That's true.'

'You know, if I think about it, there are certain things I cannot permit myself,' said Jermák, and looked up at me, his eyes brimming with tears.

'But at least I sorted everything out with Elektra. And in fact she didn't seem all that angry.'

Now Jermák burst out laughing and placed his hands on my shoulders.

'You little… Just come over here a minute! What a swan-like neck… Let's just take this off.'

He began to undo the wasp-print scarf that I had wrapped round my neck when I had set out in the biting wind. I did not reject his physical advances; let him have a Christmas present. Perhaps he likes Christmas.

'You are delicious… delicious…' he whispered in my ear.

'This is out of order. Why am I letting it happen?'

It was a rhetorical question but I expected at least a murmur by way of acknowledgement. When this failed to materialize, I opened my eyes and looked up. Jermák was standing behind me. He had twisted my hands back in such a powerful grip that it was impossible for me to move. A hard, distant sound issued from his lips:

'We are linked by ties of blood, now that we have tasted each other's. I tasted yours first, so you are in my power. You thought *you* wanted something but all the while you were doing *my* bidding.'

He leaned very close.

'I don't like victims who are passive. It's much more exciting if you resist tooth and nail…'

And with that he greedily bit into my neck.

'Ow, that hurt,' I yelled out angrily. But I was determined not to flail around, out of sheer spite.

'How do you think it works? How, you little amateur, you paper vampire! You think you can just go around biting people?

That I would just let you? I'm now going to suck you out. But properly. Pay attention and learn!'

'This is coercion! Hey! Coercion!' I tried.

'The hell it is.' Jermák spat the words out and continued to siphon off my blood.

When he finally raised his head, my life sap was dripping from his lips. He took a bottle of vodka out of his coat pocket, took a swig, gargled, and spat on the ground. He buttoned up his coat and set off. After a few steps he turned and the old supercilious smile played about his lips once more.

'I want life to be kind to you. You have become part of me. You are – you were. You were – you are. And I, I will continue to be.'

And as he said these words, he disappeared into thin air. From the spot where he had been standing, a few moments later a bat flew up, heading north-east. I lay down on the bench, my head hanging down, blood still spurting from my carotid artery on to the frozen ground. Shortly after the bat disappeared, I lost consciousness. By the morning, as a result of the loss of blood as well as the weather, which was very bitter even considering the time of the year, my body had gone completely cold.

# epilogue

THAT SAME YEAR, on a June evening, Grandma and I were sitting on the terrace of a café in the city's busiest public square enjoying the dark and the warmth. It had been only a few days since I had returned to the land of the living and everything seemed fresh and new, though I was a little depressed by the thought that as far as my friends and acquaintances were concerned I had definitively died, and even the angel had disappeared. Grandma was drinking Evian, I was reluctantly spooning a portion of strawberries and cream into my mouth. But it was no use: nothing tasted as good as when I was alive. We eyed up every passer-by, paying particular attention to young males.

Looking up from my strawberries and cream I caught sight of Jermák and Norma-Elektra cutting across the square. They didn't notice me and were deep in conversation walking at a smart pace. Grandma followed my glance and a smile of recognition spread across her face. For a few seconds she seemed to hesitate but then decided to speak:

'See, Jerne? Those people, over there. It's your mother and father.'

'What of it?' I said and with a clumsy movement managed to knock over Grandma's glass. It broke. They added the cost to our check.

**the end**

# The Finno-Ugrian Vampire, 2

## afterlife

IT SHOULD COME AS no surprise that this book is full of love. Since I have already created enough in the two major domains of literature – death and love, in that order – I hereby declare my life's work at an end.

J. V. A.

# part I

## 1

WE WERE SITTING in a café conjugating verbs when I asked her what was the link between Sachertorte and masochism. She blushed and looked away, no doubt thinking I had a dirty mind. Emboldened by this, and preferring not to give the correct answer (which happens to be an etymological curiosity), I resolved the riddle as follows:

'They are both a delicious pleasure.'

Now that I have become a vampire – it has been a year, though it feels to me much longer – I too had the desire to threaten others. This was the aim of this double entendre, too. The young woman in my company was embarrassed, so I was able to wallow intensely in my degeneracy, or at least in my filthy penchant for the frivolous. For the time being vampirism didn't come to me instinctively: I did my business with enormous effort, if at all. Perhaps this is because my sphere of interest is the human. Financial dealings, accountancy, space flight, bloodsucking – none of these had ever interested me. But the hurly-burly of everyday life, the need to meet others' expectations… Still, it had to be done. Two weeks ago I had recharged my batteries by making a woman the object of my desires, since women are in any case objects of desire and it is easier to go for something that is the way of the world than to swim against the tide. Can one, anyway, desire a man?

One can, of course, but just now it was a woman that I wanted. Not immediately, and not at any price, and not just any old one, either. I wanted to worm my way into the graces of a young, relatively intelligent Hungarian woman, so I decided I would take language lessons. This may be something of a cliché but it was an obvious solution: I would be able to benefit from an intimate relationship, regular contact and it held out the promise of revenge, for I would be able to punish her appropriately in the end for underlining in red all the mistakes in my copy book. Nevertheless, not all the liberalism and tolerance in my expensive education was enough of a safeguard against Grandma's neo-Darwinism: I had always hated ugly women. For me they are the gestures of nature most easily dispensed with; it would be better if they were all dead, for it is only beautiful flowers that are put in vases, the rest wither away unplucked. At the same time I sensed that this instinctive loathing was a good sign: the time was now not far off when I would be winging my educational way through East-Central Europe as an arrogant vampire.

My choice of language was influenced by several factors. I find the Mediterranean cultural domain by far the most congenial, but the topos of the female French teacher is very worn. Grandma argued in favour of the smaller Finno-Ugrian languages, pointing out how useful they would be on our Siberian getaways. But I really wanted to dumbfound my teacher, eventually, with my superior knowledge of the language. This latter consideration narrowed the choice down to English and Hungarian. Grandma had had me educated in an Anglo-Saxon environment for ten years, but I came out in a cold sweat at the thought of having to go through tables of the pitifully limited morphology of the English language. I also had a good grounding in Hungarian: I had written literature in Hungarian and I had also done some editing. At home, too, we mostly spoke Hungarian, and my recurrent nightmares were also dubbed in Hungarian. Why shouldn't I take up Hungarian?

Once I had taken this decision, I immediately went into action. I placed my advertisement on a board in a café frequented by intellectuals, sat down at a table nearby, ordered a glass of sparkling water, and awaited my victim. My teacher-to-be appeared within a quarter of an hour or so, read the ad, ripped it off the board and put it in her pocket with that Hungarian bravado I always find so fascinating. I put on my glasses and while she chose a table and waited to be served, I took a long look at her, because if her external appearance should prove repulsive I would rather put up another note. But the woman was good-looking and well dressed, and had barely the trace of a double chin. Her breasts were just within the intellectual range. No student could ask for more. I went home to await her call.

I discovered that very evening that my language teacher was none other than the poet O. (Let her name remain secret, as she has already had several poems published in the journal *Up-and-Coming Literature*.) I made myself out to be the child of a mixed marriage, a family that had come back to Hungary, owing my good accent to summers spent with my Hungarian grandma. In our sessions I insisted on keeping to respectable, ascetic sentence structures consisting of subject, predicate, object and at most a single complement, in case I frightened her off with my excessive competence.

After my joke about Sachertorte, O. closed the textbook with the tables of suffixes, signalling that the day's lesson was over.

'Yes, as you see, those intransitive verbs are really tricky. How did you like them, Jerne?'

'Well,' I replied slyly.

'That adverb cannot be used with the verb to like. You must respond with "very much," or "not at all" when expressing pleasure or displeasure, respectively.'

'Not very much at all. Not at all very much.'

'Still things to learn. There are subtleties, you know…'

I paid her for the session and sent a grateful glance in her direction in the hope that she would one day teach me those subtleties.

## 2

I WOULD HAVE GONE with her wherever she was headed but between 11 and 7 I had to toil away in a vegetarian restaurant with a jokey name, for a pittance. Not that I would want to suggest that carrying out the work was in any way a burden. I was prepared to take out the rubbish, use the dishwasher and deal in the traditional manner with dishes that were problematic or delicate without complaint or demur.

Still, it's worth mentioning that I was scrubbing plates by way of punishment. And I was no longer able to write stories. I was too good, you see. I had long suspected this, but it was confirmed only when Grandma gave a few of my pieces, out of sheer curiosity, to an expert. On the day of my death, Grandma had promised to have my works published privately, but she gave up this idea precisely because the expert she had consulted complimented her as follows:

'Madam, my heartiest congratulations.'

'On what?' Grandma asked.

'On the manuscript. I have to admit that your glamorous exterior would not have led me to suspect that you could both read and write.'

'I can't, not very much. But I can use a word processor.'

'Indeed. None the less, this text is outstanding. It must be published at once. It can brook no delay. Everyone must know what a skilful writer such a devilishly attractive stockbroker can be. It will be a runaway success.'

'Still, I'd like to make a few small changes.'

'It needs no changes. It needs a bit of polishing in places, of course, but that's just what makes it so charming.'

'I'd like to look over it anyway. I'll be in touch,' she said and with that swept up the manuscript and didn't stop until she got home. She tore off her sunglasses and gave me a merciless dressing-down. I remember precisely that I was in the faux-leather armchair filing down my canines because they were beginning to assume scary dimensions.

'They say you've written something good. That's not what we agreed! Do you have any idea how much that English finishing school cost me? All money down the drain!'

'I'm sorry.'

'I'm going to destroy the manuscript here and now! It could have got us into real trouble.'

I tried to think of some heart-rending plea against this course of action, though the threat did not come as a surprise. Grandma climbed on a kitchen stool and tried to find the fondue set she had been given for Christmas by her stockbroker friends, so that she could burn the papers in it, but I knew that their elimination had only symbolic value. The text awaited eternal life in several copies in my desk drawer. Still, I made a show of protesting, to ensure I didn't appear gutless.

'Please don't!'

'I certainly will. And you can take it that from now on your career as an artist is in ashes.'

'The only calling that I'm suitable for... art.'

'Have you tried anything else?'

'No. But it was you who wanted me to want this.'

She was intent on using the carrot-tale as a lighter and asked me for a match.

'I don't smoke,' I said. 'You promised I could be a writer full-time,' I added.

'Who likes full-time writers? And it's an unhealthy lifestyle, too.'

'But I cannot live without art!'

'You don't live at all any more, dearie, don't you forget. But your non-life will also have to be without art.'

'In that case I am utterly convinced that I shall never again be happy,' I snapped back. (And I never have been. Ever. But this only became clear later; not a word more about that for now. I cannot escape the linearity of the narrative.)

After this I sat for a quarter of an hour in utter silence in the faux-leather armchair, while Grandma settled on its arm beside me, massaging the nape of my neck. This kind of mechanical displacement activity probably aided her remarkable concentration.

'You are too heavy for me to hold in my lap or carry, but I think I must nevertheless tell you a little story to make you see some sense.'

'Which one?' I asked and awaited the story with uncalled-for excitement.

'The story of the cricket and the ant is one that I'm sure you know by heart, but listen to my version this time.'

'Right,' I said, as I settled myself at Grandma's feet.

'Right then. The ant was carrying out his tiresome labors, because he had a sense of responsibility and knew that his future depended solely on himself. The cricket on the other hand thought that the freedom and happiness of the individual came before everything. He played his instrument all summer long, partly because he felt he had a talent for it, partly because he enjoyed doing so. The ant, then, as I said, worked industriously, collecting seeds and crumbs, thankful for the bountiful summer. When the bitter cold of winter came, the cricket was negatively affected by two things: first his erroneous view regarding the earthly fate of creatures, and second his inability to think in the longer term, underestimating, on the basis of the summer, what the winter would be like. The ant did not mock the cricket shivering outside the anthill, only turning up a notch the volume on his radio in order not to hear his teeth chattering. When the inevitable happened he conscientiously called the beetle ambulance. The end. What is the moral of the tale?'

'Well, the presentation itself was trenchantly interpretative…'

'The moral is that anyone who lives for art should drop dead, but quietly. That's why you're going to work.'

'I like working, Grandma. I liked my work at the publisher's, it was no hardship.'

'Yes, but how about a mechanical, monotonous job this time? Manual labor would do you good. You wouldn't need to think, only to pay attention.'

I said nothing. What could some miseducated graduate with a degree in 'story writing' say to such a proposal? But Grandma then shifted into a higher gear:

'You dunderhead! You evolutionary throwback! You believed all that?' she cackled, very ear-piercingly.

I nodded to say of course I'd believed it, but I would not mind if it turned out that I had been stupid and thoughtless to do so.

'I just invented the ideological background, because I'm always capable of ideologising my proclivities. But the essence of the matter is that deep down I'm a sadistic old woman. That's why you're going to work.'

She became excited, as always, when she was about to pick a fight with me. She stood up and as she walked to and fro proceeded to give me an account of what she had come up with in her coffin.

'Wait, I've got a better idea than the cricket story. What if I handed you ready-made life goals? I'm doing your thinking for you.'

'That's even better. That breathes the spirit of the age,' I agreed.

'I've always striven not to spoil you. My fortune would have made it possible to live a life of luxury, but that would have destroyed your capacity for joy. In the depths of my soul I am an ascetic and I want you to learn that this is the true path.'

'The true path,' I echoed obediently.

'Yes. For two hundred years I lived in the lap of luxury but I have realized its vanity. Then I moved into a run-down block of apartments in Pest and I have been happy ever since. The apartment leaks, the cockroaches roam free, but I know my money is in a Swiss bank account and I can get the hell out of here anytime I want. Knowing this, you too can go and work. Treat work as your spiritual exercises.'

'You're telling me this as my grandmother?'

'No. I'm giving you knowledge from a higher spiritual plane and as a sadistic old woman.'

'I shall consider it accordingly.'

# 3

THE FOLLOWING DAY we set off to see my new employer, dressed up to the nines. A couple of phone calls and Grandma knew where my place was in this chaotic world. The restaurant sign above the dark, nitrous city-center archway was swinging in the wind, but inside we were welcomed by a blaze of light and an ecstasy of vegetables, as I could observe when I pressed my nose against the window. I could let myself go and allow myself to be enraptured into making such observations, for Grandma had persuaded them that I was her retarded niece so that they would be all the more pleased with me. The idea at first seemed absurd and later I found it was definitely in bad taste.

'How can you imagine that my intelligent looks won't give me away?'

'Put that in quotation marks!' Grandma yelped. 'Always look timid and stupid, so they don't notice how much you are their superior,' she warned me as she adjusted the cuffs of my blouse. 'That will be enough.'

The owner had known Grandma for years and was still alive. He was called Attila, and had fallen under the spell of the Eastern religions when he was at university. He became vegetarian, but in fact he opened the restaurant so that he would have a means of supplying himself and his charmingly ugly little sister with uppers and downers. The interior of the establishment was dominated by symbols of peace and visual manifestations of contempt for animal protein, though it was clear from the menu that they did use cheese and cream from self-milking cows, eggs laid by happy and liberated hens and additionally they would, on request, serve specialities made of suicidal salmon.

Attila introduced himself pleasantly and then gave me a questionnaire and asked me pleasantly to fill it in.

'Vegetarianism is not simply the eating of plants. I am also interested in the world view of my employees.'

I tackled the questionnaire while Attila quizzed Grandma about me.

'Carnivore?'

'You think I'd bring a carnivore here?'

'Because if she should stuff herself with a schnitzel roll at lunchtime that would spoil the place's karma.'

'Come now. She eats nothing but grains and water.'

'Fine. Any special peculiarities, outbursts of rage, that sort of thing?'

'No, no. She's entirely tame. You tell her what to do and she does it. Always be forceful and firm with her, to make sure her daydreaming does not impede the nimbleness of her hands.'

'I believe you. I will evaluate the questionnaire and if the result is positive, she's in,' said Attila and smiled at me encouragingly, like someone making friends with a lynx.

I wondered if he was pleased by the gentle look, the well-meaning smile with which I hid the raging wild animal, the subconscious beast in me? For my part, I took to him at once: bosses are fundamentally attractive even when they are not all that tall, handsome or intelligent.

The next day Grandma reported that Attila had called her with the news that I had got the job.

'He was spellbound by your refreshingly naïve attitude to life,' she said frostily.

As Grandma had stressed to Attila that I was incapable of co-operating effectively with anyone, I was assigned washing up duties. I could start the following day. I was not sorry. Of course, I complained effusively to Grandma about pains in my back and legs, but only so that she would not suspect what it was about my new occupation that caused me genuine agonies. Left to myself, I prefer solitary activities, so I felt as comfortable in the washing-up zone as I had in my mother's belly. Assuming, of course, that was a place that I had ever been.

# part II

## 4

WHEN HANS CHRISTIAN ANDERSEN arrived in what was then still called Pest-Buda, the first thing he did in the first bookstore he came across was buy a copy of the German translation of his breakthrough novel, *The Improvisatore*. And that's when he fell in love with this city. It is worth going all the way to Budapest to chance upon this kind of spiritual treasure. But my books will never be displayed in the store windows in this city. Because of this I felt acute self-pity in the pit of my stomach, which took the form of stabs of pain. The dry, warm weather had brought so many couples and pregnant women out on to the streets that they almost knocked me off my feet. Taken out of their natural environment in the cafés and parks, their dark mass appeared hostile.

The life goal of the writer can be nothing other than to appear in literature textbooks used in elementary and high schools. That is, there should be as many ways as possible of making available the profundities of his thought. It was for this reason especially that I regretted that I would be deprived of this possibility. The populace could not see that while I looked like a neurotic blockhead, I was in fact a wonderful free spirit. There you are. I'm agonising already. Just as Grandma had so cunningly planned.

Another reason I preferred my previous workplace was that I could get there through the City Park, while here I had to wind my way through crowded streets. But in any case we were now living somewhere else. We rented a one-bedroom apartment in the heart of the city, so that anyone looking for us would not find us in our previous residence. There was plenty of room for both of us: Grandma lived in the bedroom, I in the kitchen and bathroom. After work I hurried home to my snug little nest: three bookshelves, an armchair, a writing desk, a chair, a table and a coffin. Everything else was already on its way in containers to Helsinki.

'What about the coffin? Isn't that going to Helsinki?' I asked Grandma when I got home and saw her packing the household goods.

'No. I'll buy myself a nice new one when I'm there. I want always to have a coffin waiting for me in Hungary. So that I can feel I have not gone away for ever. They will have a National Death here yet. I have confidence in the Hungarians.'

'And I have to wait for that here?'

'Yes. Just imagine how interesting it will be to see the country rushing headlong to its destruction.'

'I'd rather go with you.'

While I trusted wholeheartedly in the blossoming of the Hungarian economy and democracy, I'm a family-loving person: if a relative of mine wants to live in a welfare state, my place is by her side.

'But didn't you tell me yesterday in the shopping center how oppressive you find this post-industrial hell?' Grandma continued, asking me to explain myself. 'If that's what it's like here, what do you expect of the decadent West?'

'I was joking.'

'Don't joke with me, my dear. Thank your lucky stars I didn't send you on a study trip to Romania,' said Grandma, bringing the exchange to a rapid close.

'But I'm a grown-up. You can't tell me where I should live.'

'Please don't bob up and down like peas on a drum for me. Pay due respect to my age.'

'Is there anything else of yours I can pay due respect to?'

'Take that back, my dear. Don't you dare talk to me like that. Me, into whose décolleté Robespierre looked deeply, to whom Franz Liszt made an indecent proposal, who almost saw Móric Jókai, whom Kierkegaard wanted to marry…'

'Kierkegaard?'

'To whom Oscar Wilde uttered an unpublished aphorism…'

'Hurry up and get to the twentieth century, Grandma.'

'The twentieth century is still too recent. But I would mention that the father of the hydrogen bomb, Edward Teller, once turned round in the street after me.'

'If you say that Thommy Berggren gave you the once over, I will kneel before you.'

'Who in death's name is he? One of the Grimm brothers' informants?'

'I'll forgive you for leaving out Thommy Berggren but the fact itself suggests a gap in your education.'

'You're being despicable. If you go on like this, one day you'll wake up to find me going for your heart with a wrought-iron candlestick. Or I'll tie a holy relic to you and then you'll rot like a pig's liver in the noonday sun.'

'That's a wholly satisfying prospect for me. There is really nothing more that I can demand of fate, if you are kind enough to perform its role,' I said, because in the interim I remembered that I wouldn't mind complete nirvana, if there was no way of obtaining work abroad.

'You should have got over these death wishes in your adolescence.'

'I was abroad then, Grandma. On my own.'

'You're being childish. But not child-like enough. And now I'm done with talking. Everything will happen as I've said, even if you're a hundred years old.'

A hundred years in Hungary? I squatted down on the floor and began to massage my temples. As I grow older, everything gets worse. I slide ever lower. Thinking back, I tried to identify the high point of my life and after a brief reflection I realized with horror that it must have been in the trauma-laden first three years of my existence.

## 5

THE COOK, who had completed high school, was aged about twenty-five and was just saying that although he did not eat meat, he could not abide Romanians, Arabs, Chinese or Gypsies. It was early in the day, the kitchen maid was chopping vegetables, while we were taking it easy as we waited for the lunchtime influx, with the day's special bubbling away in the pots.

'What about you?' he asked, turning to me.

'I hate everyone too,' I said with a bright smile, because this was the first sign of intimacy on the cook's part and I wanted to make some overtures towards my fellow workers.

'You don't have to hate everyone. Not decent Hungarian workers.'

'But I abhor them, too.'

'Get away! You're kidding, aren't you?' he exclaimed.

I retreated in confusion to the dishwasher and wondered whether all this had anything to do with the red pepper that fired up Hungarians' blood. The alkaloid in capsaicin irritates the lining of the stomach. No foreigner could ever understand the Hungarian temper without examining the local diet. The boss, an angelic-looking man with ideals, did not visit the kitchen often but in his free time gladly held training sessions for his staff. He warned the cook, for example, that he should never start work in an over-excited state, as his toxic, spiritual filth would end up cooked into the food.

6

NOVELS TELL ONE EVERYTHING worth knowing about women. Having read a large number of prose works I can safely say that in the case of women it is with their bodies that it is worth concerning oneself in detail; the rest is for collectors.

The male soul and the female body: this is what the history of the world is about. I can also briefly outline the main types: blonde women are gentle, good and kind; brunettes and dark-haired women are hot-blooded and wilful and rarely well-intentioned. Another view has it that the dark-haired ones are secretive, the redheads temperamental, the brunettes clever; the blondes, however, are not clever but cold. This too I read in books, but I believe it because it shows evidence of great insight into character.

On this evidence I was not sure what to make of O.'s dark, wavy curls, but I hoped that she dyed them. In any case I had high hopes for the best possible outcome, for O. suggested after our third meeting that we should hold our lessons in her apartment. What a woman! She has her own apartment. A dirty staircase, two rooms and hallway, worn-out carpets, a narrow, dark bathroom window giving on to the light well (I give the list in the order I encountered them).

O. was concentrating on pouring out the tea-leaf infusion, white because of the lemon and sugar, proffering it to me and meanwhile complaining in no uncertain terms about the tribulations of the novice poet. I did not like the tea, as I could only taste the boiled water, nor her plaintive remarks, but I liked O.'s breasts, this I can't deny. No detail escaped me: they swelled out from under a baby-blue pullover.

'Not too sweet?'

'Oh, not at all.' How should I know?

'But this is far too sugary. Let's add some milk.'

She did so and continued her moan. I couldn't understand what was causing her pain, as I thought the Hungarians liked beautiful young women poets as long as they didn't have any children and sometimes even if they did. Of course O.'s beauty manifested itself only in relation to her poetic status.

'Out of a hundred people only two read poetry. What about you, Jerne? Do you ever read poetry?'

'No.'

'Really?' she asked, frightened. 'Perhaps you don't understand Hungarian poems?'

'I do. But I have no soul.'

'I wonder what you mean by that. Perhaps you have no sensitivity to the lyrical?'

'Could be.'

'Perhaps you haven't tried the right poems. Poetry is one of the most wonderful things. It's enchanting. I, for example, always think of poetry even when I am having an orgasm.'

'I don't.'

I dipped my tongue in the hot water and realized straight away that this was no way to seduce a woman poet. I started again:

'I'm not thinking of poetry as such. What I have in mind is literature as a whole. L-I-T-E-R-A-T-U-R-E. In golden block capitals, like Metro-Goldwyn-Mayer.'

'Sounds interesting. I'll have to try it.'

I put on one of my most sympathetic smiles as I feverishly scoured the unused areas of my brain for a neutral topic. I wondered whether O. was actually stupid or just had an adaptive nature. She was the first to remember why we were actually there:

'Well then… What was the homework for today?'

'The family.'

I read out my appalling little composition. Father, mother, brothers and sisters, domestic bliss.

'It's short but amusing,' said O.

'My real family is boring.'

'It is a curious aspect of your linguistic skills that you commit more errors in your writing than in your conversation.'

'That's because I have time to think.'

And how much care I had lavished on this composition! First I wrote it out in English, then I translated it back word for word into Hungarian, but refining it a little: for example I omitted the copula 'to be' in three places, the first person pronoun and some other little affectations of the agglutinating language, but I left in a few, just to give it all some flavor. I mixed up the endings on the two conjugations wherever possible, because that is really effective.

'Yes, perhaps in situations needing an immediate response, the Hungarian language you heard in the cradle instinctively comes to the surface.'

'Exactly.'

'I appreciate your efforts. Hungarian is one of the most difficult languages, and from an objective point of view completely useless. You, too, are learning it for personal reasons, aren't you?'

'Of course,' I replied and aimed my standard hypnotic glance firmly in the direction of O. I will get into this vampire business, like an ox learns to plough, I assured myself as O. leaned back in her chair with a shudder of horror.

7

GRANDMA'S LAST FEW DAYS had been spent in a frenzy, buying up Hungarica absolutely essential for survival overseas.

'How could I live without this?' she kept muttering as she laid out before me on the table acacia honey, goose liver, Tokaji wine and Kalocsa red pepper. I couldn't really understand why she would not be able to manage without these foodstuffs, but even the thought of asking her about it exhausted me. It's some kind of state secret, I decided. I was lolling about on the sofa with a notebook in my lap and watching the energetic *femme fatale*. She was dashing to and fro as she packed; she had a ticket for a flight to Helsinki the next day. In the middle of it all, she suddenly looked at me and said casually:

'When I was in town I bumped into your father. He was with a good-looking eighteen-year-old lad.'

'How do you know he was eighteen? Was his date of manufacture stamped on him?' I snapped back. To hear this about my father made me feel exactly the way little Alice must have felt when she was no longer ten years old and Lewis Carroll no longer gave her a second look. Unpleasant, but it did not cut me to the quick.

'Why shouldn't I know his age? Maybe I held the candle when he was born.'

'I'm sure you know many things, Grandma. Do you know, for example, how to seduce a woman?'

'You're still at that stage?'

'I've never done it. Help me.' I really didn't know how to do it. I had covered two pages with flow charts and sentences that I thought might work.

'If you are interested in the verbal side, you could have a look at these,' Grandma said and from the cardboard boxes destined to be thrown away she fished out a bundle of letters tied up with pack thread.

'Love letters? You had love affairs?'

'Not on my side. But from the outside doubtless that's what it looked like, whatever the approach may have been. The point is that in the end, I won. I distracted them and then stabbed them in the back. That's how vampires always do it.'

'I know,' I nodded, and opened the letters.

'I'll tell you how it was,' she began energetically, as she color-sorted her knickers into the various sections of her valise. 'This fellow wrote letters because he was not as tall as me. That is a serious flaw in a man, almost unforgiveable.'

I had meanwhile spread out the colored pieces of paper in my lap.

'Or wasn't it that one? Show me the handwriting. Or the signature. For a moment I thought that was the weedy-looking mathematician who had a really hard time. But no. This is someone else. I can't remember his name, unfortunately.'

'Your loving…'

'Don't you dare read them out or I'll puke. Filthy intimacies make my stomach turn. Of course I know who it is. I know my way around the more recent ones, but before the telephone became commonplace I had to employ a secretary to deal with my correspondence. I threw out the envelopes from that time long ago: they were full of locks of hair and pressed flowers; keeping those is unhygienic.'

I read parts of some of the letters and noted down on slips of paper on the little telephone table any turns of phrase that I found appealing.

'Grandma, you really allowed people to embrace you?'

'Being a vampire seems like all glitter from the outside, but it has a few disgusting concomitants. That's what makes the telephone such a wonderful invention. And that's why I have invested half my fortune in telecommunication technologies, to make sure the love letter dies out. Nothing except contracts are worthy of enduring for more than a few months. Every trace of lovers' mewlings has a damaging cumulative effect on the universe. I, too, have a responsibility for the Earth, I have to make it a better place, for I shall be living here a hundred, and even a thousand, years from now.' Grandma packed away all the black underwear and banged the lid of the valise shut. 'Well, have you found anything?'

'Yes, I've copied out four extracts.'

'Which ones? Read them out.'

'"My life has become thick with you. This is what I have secretly longed for." I detected the topos of the forbidden fruit. "The way you look at me. Mm! That is impossible to read." That *Mm*! is so evocative and suggestive of orgasmic delight. "You are very inspiring. Beautiful and thought-provoking." That links aesthetic and intellectual values. Clever. And the last one: "Yield your body to the irrational and to me".'

'You see, the brain is always left out in the end. You see how interesting it is, Jerne? In places irresistibly amusing and at the same time elevated. I think that in those few weeks he poured all his intellectual capacities into these letters. If you like them, feel free to use them. No copyright fee.'

'Thank you, Grandma.'

'Or you can keep looking in that box. It's full of genuine feeling.'

I lay down on my stomach on the kitchen sofa – which is where I slept so as not to invade Grandma's personal sphere – and started plotting. I had so much material about love that I could easily have written a romantic duet about the eldest son of the influential Gopher and the poverty-stricken young female rabbit. I allowed my thoughts to entertain this topic only out of amusement, for I was not allowed to write stories. Yet I had already imagined the scene where the grey-haired Gopher tries to dissuade his son from marrying beneath himself.

'But Father,' the son would say, 'of your 1,240 descendants why should I be the only one not allowed to choose a partner after my heart?'

'You must understand, you dimwit, that the two of you cannot reproduce and that is one of the most powerful organising principles of Nature.'

'And does mutual sympathy count for nothing? In that case, Father, I am ready to give up the custom of my ancestors for the sake of a higher organising principle: love,' the boy would say, and storm out slamming the gopher-hole door behind him.

Forbidden love that conquers all is the king of topoi and I had succeeded in striking the right note. If I read a little more specialist literature I would be able to make my animal heroes feel the faith of love with conviction. Why am I so unbearably wise? Because I have died, or because I do so much dishwashing? I would write stories, modelling them on *Bambi* and *Bambi's Children*, a series called *Initiative* and *Initiative's Children*. The gopher's son would, alas, die at the end, his head smashed in by the edge of the spade of a gopher exterminator from the next village. A kind of anti-gopher pogrom, because they had devoured the crop. But I knew in this form it was not suitable for children.

As if adults were not sufficiently mature to accept the tragedy that the fulfilment of desires means. This is why you have to deal with them gently: it is better if you give them stories that end unhappily. Their souls fall to pieces with the resolution, but it is understandable: what a huge vacuum is left behind! It is a burden that only a healthy child's soul is capable of bearing. I had been carried away by ardor, but hardly had I written down the address on the sheet of paper when Grandma burst in, shaking her head:

'No, Jerne. No, no. You know, when you were small that's what I said to you when you were about to put your fingers in the light socket. But these days I'm beginning to think that it was a pity I intervened.'

'No what?'

'Put down pen and paper. For the time being you can't write. Only when you have acquired sufficient experience of life. Lie down and rest; you've had a hard day.'

Obediently I lay down and Grandma covered me up.

'That's right. Don't think about anything. Or think of me! That's always nice,' she said and turned off the light.

# 8

LEANING SLIGHTLY FORWARD, supporting myself against the bar, I scanned the day's news. Our eatery subscribed to all the important party dailies, because our clientele attracted plant-eaters of every political hue. Meanwhile I was keeping an eye on Attila as he totted up the figures for the day's turnover. If our glances met, he would quickly return his gaze to the columns of figures and with his artistic hands keep stabbing demurely at the numbers on his pocket calculator. I amazed myself: what a steep learning curve I was on – in the end even I would make my mark on the universe, dreaded equally by man and woman.

Behind my back, the cook was sharing a joint with the waiter while performing extracts from the children's opera *Wonderlawn*, in which he must have shone, before his voice broke, in the role of some dynamic forest hobgoblin. He even performed a few dance steps and I was beginning to wonder how the spinach and leek tart would make it to the diners' tables when an excited conversation filtering in from the entrance reached our ears. A couple of minutes later it transpired that the problem was of such magnitude that the boss had to be called.

'It grabbed it just a minute ago.'

'It's eating it. Eating it!' came the whispers from outside.

The ornithological expertise of the three of us – though in my case, as a writer of animal stories, I ought to know at least something about birds as well – proved inadequate at identifying exactly the species of the bird, but it was a safe bet that some fairly large bird of prey was just consuming an urban pigeon behind the restaurant, on the concrete inner courtyard of the block of apartments. An unappreciative audience gaped through the French windows at the bloody scene.

Attila dropped his ballpoint and dashed forward. He was determined: broomstick in hand, he indicated unmistakeably to the bird that its presence was not desired. The latter was taken aback by Attila's spirited stand and departed with its slit-stomached booty and without further ado.

'How disgusting,' huffed Attila afterwards and shook his broomstick in our direction, too, like some minor but – within his sphere of influence – all-powerful god shaking his trident. 'I can only think that the spirituality of our restaurant is inadequate. And since I can see no crack in the armor of my own convictions, I suspect that it is one of you that doubts that this path leads to pure knowledge. Someone has made a gaping, bloody wound on a body cleansed of toxins and the bird of prey was lured here by its smell.'

I bowed my head, hardly able to bear the reproachful look that suggested I had scored a bloody wound on the snow-white body of vegetarianism. Yet I could barely recall the last time I tasted blood. Vampirism, just like literature, is not something to be denied.

Following Attila's departure the cook again took charge and launched into a rendering of the folk song that begins 'My golden carriage is pulled by two swans...'

'Join in!' he urged me with a wink in my direction.

'I don't know the words,' I said and closed the door behind me. I did not appreciate Attila's latest attempt at a loyalty programme, namely the adding to our monthly pay of two grams of rather good quality dried wild hemp. And I continued to worry how the spinach and leek tart would find its way on to our diners' tables.

# 9

WHEN IT CAME TO WOMEN and especially so-called clever women, I was still rather short of creative ideas. The effectiveness of Grandma's love letters on a so-called clever woman appeared predictable and indeed appreciable, but then we know well that this is not enough. What kind of thing makes them happy? What do they want to listen to? What are they unable to resist?

These days it is not enough to say to a woman 'you have lovely eyes'. Love poems addressed to their person might possibly have done the trick, but O. knew too much about poetic meter. Much more, for sure, than me, a depressingly prosaic soul. Grandma is always boasting about how no one ever resisted her for longer than a week. Anyone who held out longer, she married and never bit his neck.

A month passed and still I had not got beyond the preparatory stage; indeed, I couldn't even decide whether O. was really not beautiful but seemingly intelligent, or beautiful but seemingly unintelligent. Perhaps she was beautiful and clever? Ugly and stupid? A clever woman? A beautiful woman? It was by no means irrelevant what kind of material I was working with. Though I might not have been certain, I had, however, discerned several times on O.'s face that she would have liked to talk of her love life. In the end she dared to risk this for the first time after we had known each other for two weeks.

She opened the door after letting the bell ring for a long time, and launched straight into the following:

'Forgive me, I may be very distracted today, but I'm rather upset.'

I gave her an understanding smile, for if she was rather upset, she was allowed to be very distracted.

'I'm reluctant to say why, but next month it will be six months since, after five months' stressing about it, I had a week-long affair with a former teacher of mine. Ever since my heart has been pounding.'

'Ever since?'

'No. No, no. Only because I've just seen him again. I was walking along the street. In the pedestrian zone. I was wearing my red skirt. Do you think it suits me? I'd just gone into the chemist's… No, it was before I got to the chemist's, but I could see the store sign. That's when I came face to face with him.'

I undid my shoelaces with great empathy.

'I said "Hello" and then he said "Hello" and then he went on his way. Or rather, they went on theirs, because he was with his wife.'

'He's married?' I asked, to reassure O. I was following her train of thought.

'Yes. With three children.'

I looked up.

'But they are very small. And the whole thing lasted only a week. In fact, the smallest was still inside his mummy's tummy at the time.'

'I don't think that's very nice.'

'You don't?' O. was taken aback.

It was something I suspected, rather than thought. How would I know? Then I remembered a novel that offered a lifeline.

'But it's understandable. Men's lives are harder than women's. They have to resort to external resources, because they don't have inexhaustible internal resources like women do,' I said slowly, as if I was just making it up on the spot and looking for the right words.

This failed to console O. She had succeeded in embarrassing herself, too, with her honesty and now she just stood by the shoe rack, crumpling the edge of her little flowery shirt. I decided to show more empathy; that always does the trick.

'If you feel like writing a poem now... and want me to leave... it's no problem... I'll come tomorrow.'

'No, it's all right. I can hold back a little longer,' she said, trying to regain her composure. 'I have some very interesting exercises for you. Come on. Oh, how many times have I told you there's no need to take your shoes off indoors.'

I followed her into the inside room. As I looked at her bare legs, and her hands as she scratched her unkempt hair from time to time, it occurred to me that this was something that someone might, in fact, like.

# 10

I DON'T LIKE saying goodbyes because I find it very boring and it prompts people to make embarrassing declarations. We arrived at the airport, Grandma and I, so early that there was time for her to ask me to demonstrate that I had 'moral fiber' even when she was not there. This made a cold sore appear on the left part of her upper lip. This despite the fact that I had told her any number of times to choose her words carefully.

'All you have to say is that I should obey your instructions, that's enough for me, there's no need to use high-flown language, particularly as you know you're allergic to it,' I berated her with great glee.

'But moral fiber has never given me a sore before, only love of mankind.'

'Grandma, before you go, I'd like to ask you something.'

'Go ahead.'

'I just wanted to know whether you have read my pieces?'

'Yes, I leafed through the manuscript while waiting for a client.'

'And?'

'I quite liked it, but…'

'But?'

'For my taste it contains too many letter *a*'s.'

'Letter *a*'s?'

'Yes. It needs more *e*'s, and there aren't enough *i*'s either. You must pay attention to vowel harmony. Not *i* and *é*, those are neutral, as you know. But where there is *a*, there should be *o*, *ó* or *á*. For anyone writing in Hungarian, it's a matter of conscience. On the whole.'

Grandma's flight came up on the board and I was very glad that the intensive course on the art of writing was over.

'Listen, Jerne. I put two cans of tinned blood on the top shelf of the kitchen cabinet. But don't touch it unless you are in dire straits. That's all I could get. There was no more to be had for love or money. And I'm not strong enough to raid the National Blood Transfusion Center on my own.'

'Kitchen cabinet, top shelf,' I repeated.

'But if you scoff the lot within a month, you'll starve. Don't you dare die on me while I'm working in Finland. There's that little Hungarian language teacher. You'll have her, won't you?'

'I will, of course.'

'Minimum. The task is to suffer, suffer and suffer but not starve to death.'

# part III

# 11

IF I LOOK BACK on the past, the most delirious moments of joy for me came about when I was able to have food in my mouth. I must, after all, be grateful for being one of the living dead and not feeding in the traditional manner, for what I earned could only pay for my rent and the outgoings. Thanks to a fortunate coincidence, however, it would not have been a problem had I still needed to eat. At my place of work there were sackfuls of leftovers and kitchen waste by the bucketful. Sometimes, for the sake of the oral ritual of eating, I would stuff into my mouth a slice of pie, lonely on a returned plate. For I could still recall the wonderful taste of curd cheese with raisins.

Grandma looked after me with exemplary care. She had locked my money away for a hundred years, it's true, to motivate me to maintain the vampirical way of life, but if I behave according to her instructions, the bank deposit will be mine within a generation and a half, and that's more than tempting. Indeed, she did her bit for contemporary culture too: she insisted that my small stipend was spent on the arts to the last penny, with receipts to prove it.

I discovered that in Grandma's books I was registered as a 'cultural receptor' – Grandma had a penchant for pseudo-Latin terminology – while Uncle Oscar was down to receive a daily hot meal as 'applied aesthete'. Uncle Oscar has not been mentioned so far and this is unjust. He came to the restaurant every day to consume the special of the day. If we weren't too busy I could break off from washing up for half an hour. I would wipe my sodden hands reeking of washing-up liquid in my apron and take him his meal.

Uncle Oscar had fled the standard American dream for the sophisticated, gently plaintive culture of Central Europe, whereas some decades earlier his grandparents had traveled in the opposite direction. The frequent, self-revelatory conversations conducted with him suggested that Uncle Oscar's trajectory had led from a suburban house (and not any old where, either: next door to where Norman Mailer used to beat his wife) through teaching institutions maintained for New Yorkers' depraved millionaire offspring and Los Angeles student protests to a doctorate in England and then a hospital in Amsterdam where Oscar, who had been sent there after taking an overdose, thought he recognized in the nurse leaning over him a member of the heavenly host. Quite apart from the enumeration of the events of his significant and radical youth, every meal I spent with him was enjoyable. It was enough for me to watch him as he ate our dishes, top-quality and preservative-free. For example, that day, potato balls with apple and red cabbage.

'You're not eating?'

'No. For me, I find it's enough to watch. I see so much food,' I added hurriedly and put my hand on his shoulder encouragingly.

Why shouldn't I put my hand on his shoulder, why shouldn't I watch him eating red cabbage: I had known him since I was a child. I was just twelve the summer that he began to pay his attentions to Grandma. Of the several hundred men whom I could recall Grandma having relations with, Oscar stood out by virtue of the fact that he was the only one who did not ignore me. For instance, if on a bright summer morning he rang our bell, and Grandma was still resting in her coffin, he would take me by the hand for a walk in the awakening city.

'Look at those self-aware proletarians!' he would say, pointing to the dustmen and street cleaners going about their business.

He quickly grew very close to my child-like heart, so I asked him to marry the adult belonging to me.

'Your mother is a beautiful woman, but I'm gay,' he replied.

At the time I was not yet very good at Hungarian, so I couldn't understand the relationship between cause and effect, but the word 'but' suggested that this was a rejection of my suggestion. So he didn't become my daddy then, but there was a sudden gleam of hope now, since before she went off Grandma had designated Uncle Oscar as my spiritual mentor. Though when I miraculously found my parents I was touched by the repetitive complexity of life, I strove to forget about them as quickly as possible. My creed is: new story – new daddy. Uncle Oscar himself made me promise not to hesitate to turn to him should I have trouble with the analysis of a work of art, or have a problem of a metaphysical nature.

After he had taken five or six mouthfuls and chewed and swallowed them at a leisurely pace, he gave me an inquiring look.

'I went to a performance piece yesterday,' I replied slowly.

'The one I recommended?'

'No, another. The performance artist first belabored us with a classic historical monodrama, then, having tested the patience and endurance of the audience for forty-five monotonous minutes, simply sat at the edge of the stage and began to tell the story of his life. It was very good, personal.'

'Sounds good.'

'It was. At the beginning I wanted to run out of the theater, but my feet were so sore, it felt good to be sitting down. I stayed. And by the end it got quite good.'

'Jerne, let me tell you something. It distresses me the way your mother, whom I otherwise hold in high esteem, allows you to languish away like this.'

'She just wants to teach me how to behave…'

'Let me finish. My grandmother is one hundred and six years old.'

Mine is two hundred and thirty five. Nevertheless I tried hard to register the information with a surprised expression.

'Can you imagine it? One hundred and six. And she is still alive. She is sitting on mountains of money and I am designated as sole heir in her will. It's no secret: I expect to hear the good news any day now. You don't think me unfeeling, do you?'

'No. One hundred and six is truly superhuman.'

'Yes, and it's over the top as well. At least from my point of view. But why am I telling you all this? As soon as I inherit the money, I'll make you a gift of some of it, so that you can live by yourself, independently.'

'I wouldn't accept it.'

'You will, as it will not mean any special burden for me.'

'OK, I will accept it.'

Uncle Oscar went on with his meal. To the word 'dessert', uttered with a questioning intonation, he gestured no, so I only poured some water in his glass. He took a sip and asked:

'Have you read any books lately?'

'No, I've just looked through some magazines. Poems about relationships where all feeling is gone…'

'Ah.'

'Uncle Oscar, when did you last speak with my mother?'

'Yesterday or the day before. I tried unsuccessfully to persuade her of the futility of trying to teach people a lesson. She insists on believing that thanks to the pains of washing up you'll learn to value the advantages of the way of life she recommends.'

'I, too, can hardly wait to reach that breaking point.'

'If things should come to such a pass, my advice would be never to be ashamed of crying. Don't hesitate to cry!'

'Should the opportunity present itself, I certainly will, but now out of loyalty to the firm I must ask whether you would like some more cabbage. Our seasonal offer: for only a small supplement we can offer every regular a second helping of steamed cabbage.'

'I won't say no. Thank you.'

Uncle Oscar leaned back in his chair and pushed an unruly tuft of hair back behind one ear. I was truly pleased that he had asked for cabbage. Ever since his father had disowned him aged twenty and he had lived off occasional sums of money from his mother, he did not consider it beneath his dignity to freeload, to take advantage of price cuts and seasonal price reductions.

The sheer quantity of that cabbage! The amount! The regulars had now been munching their way through it for a second week. Our buyer operated on the principle that food is not to be thrown out – he came from a Protestant family with many children, apart from which he had invested a sizeable sum in the business – and all this manifested itself in the discounted dispensing of cabbage and cabbage salad. The cook was constantly flustered and agitated, making cheese-filled cabbage rolls and cabbage stuffed with tofu.

'Here you are. It's really good.' I put the cabbage down in front of Uncle Oscar, who was sitting calmly at the corner table, like a rich aphorism manufacturer.

'Won't you sit with me?' he asked.

'You know I'm working.'

'All right, off you go then. See you later,' and Uncle Oscar's fork ploughed into the cabbage heap.

# 12

MY ATTEMPTS to entrap and drain O. – to which I gave the anthropological *terminus technicus* 'fieldwork' – had recently been made easier by some theoretical spadework I had done. Though no specific work of literature actually declared this from the many allusions to it, the universal principle emerged with considerable clarity. I'm referring to the *theory of time-wasting*. I will not go into the possibility that is commonly referred to as *love at first sight*, because the theory applies exclusively to situations where, on the occasion of the first encounter, there still exists the 'slight antipathy' that Nietzsche also alludes to in one of his works. Since this last can be dispelled, it's all a matter of getting attuned to it. Man is an addictive creature. The reason that this is a source of joy for me is that it makes it possible to develop dependencies in O. even in the absence of attractive qualities on my part, provided I wave at her at every turn in the road. My physical actuality will fill the yawning gap in her soul, which she has hitherto filled with other substitutes.

I even compiled a chart. Vertical axis: method, example, intention (mine), effect (on her). The rubrics of the line marked intention featured time-wasting all the way. In places also, of course: shared experiences. Naturally, if I wanted to give a more nuanced account of this fieldwork, I would detail the significance of the latter, too, but let this be a sketchy introduction for the time being, indicative of the most characteristic feature.

'How many mixed metaphors so far?' I asked looking up from the composition that had been given as homework.

'Not more than three,' O. assured me. 'Don't worry, I've had more idiotic students than you.'

'Good to know.'

'He bombarded me unremittingly for a week, begging me not to deny him my favors. Of course I wrote him a tough letter of rejection. I'm very proud of that letter, it was written entirely in the style of the Anglo-Saxon essay, with the thesis: "You surely don't imagine you can bed me?"'

'Forgive me for interrupting, but a question can't be a thesis.'

'No? In that case that might be why I didn't manage to convince him. This despite the fact that I ended my argument with a quote from Goethe: "The tragedy begins when the frivolous comedy is over".'

'A powerful quotation…'

'Isn't it? I thought so, too.'

'…but the correct form of the thesis would be "You will not bed me", to be followed by the arguments for and against.'

'All right, but I won't tolerate any further undermining of my authority as a teacher. Let's correct your composition!' O. said imperiously.

While I read out the ambiguous sentences, full of confused metaphors – I had copied them from newspapers – what kept thundering in my head was motivation, motivation. And where I was going to find it. Could I hope that the time would come when we would be consumed by passion? Sometimes I felt O. was very close to me. When I was alone, lying on my back or side, I frequently summoned up her image. More recently I had taken her into my dreams as well.

# 13

I WAS ONCE AGAIN sitting on the dishwasher. Attila had asked me to promise by everything that was sacred that I would no longer sit on the dishwasher. But to me nothing is sacred. Nor do I have any goodwill, because he had also said 'if you had an ounce of goodwill, you wouldn't sit on the dishwasher again.'

A friendly smell of cooked vegetables hung about the place. The cook was having a destructive day that no vitamin would survive: he cooked and boiled the vegetables, shaped them into little balls before frying them in oil at 200 degrees. If Attila were to see this, his heart would skip a beat, I thought, but Attila had got out of the wrong side of the bed and only looked into the kitchen in passing before going back home to shoot up.

'Have you washed up the big pot from yesterday?' asked the cook as he put his head round the door.

'I have indeed,' I said, looking up from my book.

Since I had got to know O., I read only kitschy trash in order to maintain a heightened awareness of the romantic. Within this range, I had begun to acquire a curiously soft spot for very light reading from the interwar period: I was just reading about a shorthand typist who had hit the jackpot.

'Then wash up today's as well!'

I was quite certain that the secretary's boss would in the end marry the girl destined for higher things. But how would he get over the fact that Manci was no unused ticket, as it were? Annoyed, I jumped off the dishwasher.

'By the way, in my opinion Carthage must be destroyed,' I said, because it is one of my principles that Greco-Roman civilisation is the spice of daily life.

'Shut it!' muttered the cook as he flung the pot at me.

He has a heart of gold otherwise, but there was something oppressing his heart. The vitamins were well on their way to annihilation and the green beans had been burnt as well. There was something fierce in the man's personality, even though he had served his apprenticeship at a Hare Krishna soup kitchen with a specialisation in vegan food. In my view it was not religious conviction, merely his desire to learn and his love of the profession that had taken him down this career path.

'Shall I put up on the board that today's special is green beans in a piquant sauce?' I asked affably, at the same time offering him an opportunity, so to speak, to ease his soul. Though he did sometimes tear me off a strip, deep down the cook liked me because I didn't talk a lot and watched his every word wide-eyed.

'Do,' he agreed. 'You are the only one in this place who understands me.'

And that was indeed the case.

From the back window I could see Uncle Oscar tottering towards the restaurant. He was neither drunk, nor even slightly tipsy; the manner of his locomotion was solely a consequence of his height. I ran towards him but first wrote up on the board: 'Chef's special: tender green beans in a delicate piquant sauce', managing to imbue it with a touch of literary creativity.

'I'd like some of that,' Uncle Oscar said.

'There isn't any,' I said because I didn't want to cause this father figure of mine any unhappiness.

'But you've just written that on the sign.'

'There isn't any... yet.'

'Then I don't want anything. How are you today, Jerne?'

'Really unwell.'

'This is absurd! Why do you always give a straight answer? You have to observe the rules of conversation. You must reply "Thank you, I'm fine." Then I suggest "But you don't look well. Is anything the matter?" This was something my grandfather taught me, he knew what good manners are.'

'Do I look unwell?'

'Always. You have a distinctly harassed look.'

'Shall I give you a smile, Uncle Oscar?'

'Don't bother. I'd rather hear what you've been reading.'

'Nothing. Nothing worth mentioning.' I was convinced Uncle Oscar could not approach my populist deviation with the requisite irony.

'Come on, out with it. When you get home after a hard day's work, you only want to read something light,' he said and you could tell he was not joking.

'Sometimes not even that. I lie on my back, stare at the ceiling, and reflect on my wasted life for half an hour. By then I'm asleep.'

'The working class has all my sympathies, but this really will not do.'

'I want to read stories. Those are really entertaining.'

'It escapes my understanding that you always want to be entertained,' snapped Uncle Oscar. 'Is this a fairground? It's a wholly reactionary attitude.'

I fell silent and gnawed my fingernails. Uncle Oscar took a newspaper from his jacket pocket and ostentatiously buried himself in its pages.

'Listen, Uncle Oscar. It's the end of the month and I still have 20,000 forints to spend on culture. What the hell am I to do?'

'Buy tickets to the opera! Two for today, two for tomorrow,' he said but without looking up from his paper. He turned a page, still reading intently.

I hung around him for a while not knowing what to do, then I sat down and looked at him pleadingly.

'I'm sick of all this garbage about the holocaust,' he suddenly exclaimed and crumpled up the newspaper.

'Me too,' I rejoined timidly, hoping I might placate him by agreeing.

'What?' he snorted. 'Let me not hear any anti-Semitic talk! This is a personal matter, for me as a Jew.'

And so he left me sitting at the corner table of the vegetarian restaurant with a jokey name at 4.00 in the afternoon.

# 14

I SPENT the whole afternoon fretting that Uncle Oscar and I were not singing from the same hymn-sheet. To try to placate him I started to read two of the books he had recommended, and copied out turns of phrase from a volume of essays: 'my education shackles me', 'the writer strives to disturb my usual little world', 'language is a false channel of communication'. When I was done with this, I folded some money into my trouser pocket and with slow, measured steps walked over to the opera. I watched the opera-lovers as they gathered, and as their exquisite excitement also engendered in me a desire for bel canto, I decided that as soon as I had the opportunity I would buy tickets to the opera. I would have preferred to hear at once the squawk of double-chinned old ladies and fifty-year-old lyric tenors. I had always considered opera an artificial genre but, perhaps precisely for this reason, extremely appealing. This time I preferred to go to another part of town and waste O.'s time.

It was only about 8.00 in the evening when I rang her doorbell, but O. received me in her nightdress.

'Come in, come in,' she trembled in a somewhat sedated voice. 'You've come at just the right time, as I'm very much alone. It's possible that your sheer presence is preventing me from committing suicide.'

'That would be wonderful,' I said good-humoredly and sat down in an armchair draped in female underwear.

Artists need depression like a fish needs water: before, after, instead. I'd like to linger over the underwear, too. Hats off: I liked what she wore next to her skin, I was pleased she had spread them out before me.

'A lovely pair of lace knickers,' I said lifting one up in some confusion.

'And it looks good on me, too,' she said dryly and then put a shot glass in front of me. 'You know, Jerne, it's my birthday in six weeks' time. Let's have some vodka.'

'All a woman needs is a sugar boost, not to get drunk.'

'But I'm going to have some vodka anyway,' said O. 'Ever since my twenty-second I haven't been able to stand birthdays.'

'But it's still six weeks away,' I argued, making use of the piece of information she had just supplied.

'I'm already in mourning.'

'How are you in mourning?' I asked out of sheer curiosity.

'I don't believe in anything except alcohol and medicines, the only items whose composition is permanent.'

'How true! I can't imagine a more beautiful death either,' I said approvingly.

'You'll have one with me, of course.' O. poured the liquid into the little shot glasses.

I looked around to see if there was a houseplant nearby that could absorb a thimbleful.

'Down the hatch.'

I wouldn't like to give the false impression that the Hungarians are alcoholic to a man (or woman). That's out of the question. For many people, however, alcohol is a part of daily life. Not long ago Grandma wrote to me saying that she did not dare bite into a neck on Fridays, Saturdays or Sundays, because she had landed on the floor more than once after a suck or two. But once she had taken the measure of the Finns' drinking habits, she knew there would be no problems. One has to know when to suck. With the Hungarians? Well, here you can never tell. There are no set days. That day, for example, was a Wednesday and O. was already pouring herself her second. However, the glass before me was still full. I tried to weigh up whether, if I sent O. to the kitchen claiming that I would not touch it without salt and lemon and I might be able to empty it on to the ficus plant and then say I'd decided to knock it back suddenly after all, she would see through the cheap ploy. So instead I accidentally tipped over the glass.

'That's OK. It'll dry. I'll pour you another.'

As she did so, she spoke:

'A few weeks ago, for the umpteenth time, I was arguing with my friends about the effect of various mood-altering substances on increasing creativity. The arguments that flew about! You couldn't imagine how many genuine fans there are of cheap plonk!'

'I don't think so.'

'What do you mean you don't think so?' She gave me an odd look.

'I don't.'

'You misunderstood. I didn't ask a question. It's good to know that you can misunderstand things. Sometimes I get the feeling there's nothing more I can teach you.'

'From you one can only learn. You're a poet, after all.' I was licking deep and wet.

'Come now,' she bridled. 'You haven't yet read a single poem of mine. I may be a bad poet. Though I wouldn't say so myself. I'm good. Experienced at being a woman.'

'What else do you know?' I asked without the slightest curiosity.

'Oh...' she began.

'I've just realized that I have an unbearable headache. I have to go,' I decided suddenly, as I noticed O. was again reaching for the bottle.

In five or ten minutes I could have done with her whatever I wanted, but on the one hand I have a sense of pride and on the other I am a teetotaller. A victim with this level of alcohol in her would have a worse effect on my chaste system than on Grandma's much more practised body. No. Not today, not at any price. Perhaps tomorrow, the following day or next week.

# part IV

# 15

ON A WARM SPRING AFTERNOON I was sitting on a bench by the bank of the Danube writing in my canvas-bound notebook. Not far from me the promenade's young Romanian male prostitutes were sunning their fresh faces in the golden rays of the setting sun, their merry prattle reaching even my ears. The idyllic nature of the scene began to weigh on me and I would have left, had Uncle Oscar not designated this spot for our rendezvous. It was the first afternoon of a long weekend.

Soon Uncle Oscar arrived and one could see that the cloudless sky and sunshine had confused him, too, with regard to nature's intentions towards mankind.

'How spring-like it is!' he rejoiced. 'May I sit down? What are you writing?'

'A novel. But at the moment I'm just taking notes.'

'Make sure you put me in it too. These days you can't really have a novel without a gay man in it. Let me be the understanding homosexual friend that the hero can always count on. Even in trouble.'

'Fine. Done.'

'Your mother of course instructed me always to intervene if I saw you writing. But I won't tell her, don't worry.'

I wanted to hug his neck, so overcome with joy was I at this easing of my wholly justified paranoia. I suddenly had the feeling that I needed to share something important with this dear man.

'Listen, Uncle Oscar, what would you say… if we took each other by the hand and drowned ourselves in the Danube?'

'You mean jump off the Chain Bridge?'

'If you like.'

'I don't feel like it today. The sunshine is so wonderful today,' Uncle Oscar shrugged.

'I'm surprised that you are turning me down. Your basic nature is, after all, suicidal.'

'Yes, but last time I felt sorry for the fire-fighters when they had to talk someone down from the statue of our mythical Turul bird.'

'That's not the Chain Bridge.'

'Jerne, I'm sorry, but you've been talking nonsense non-stop for the last few minutes. I'm over fifty years old and the prospect of receiving a vast sum of money is on the horizon. Your situation is shit, I can see that but don't project your depression on to me. I can bear this life even if I have to stand on one foot.'

'At least I know where we both stand.'

'I'll tell you how it works: don't expect things to get steadily better, because they won't, they'll get steadily worse. I am a half-blood: my mother is Jewish, my father Catholic. I mention this because from this point of view there's not much to choose between them. For a long time I too thought that all injustice and suffering was either justified or deserved being compensated for. But I have now grown used to the idea that the universe has no ombudsman of human fate. If the weather is overcast today, there is no guarantee that tomorrow the sun will shine.'

'In this light, what is to be done?'

'Let's lean back and enjoy the sun,' said Uncle Oscar and for his part did just that.

I was reminded of sheep, because these days I had sheep, rather than bees, in my bonnet. I got up, determined to leave.

'Where are you off to?' Uncle Oscar said opening one eye.

'Just off.'

'But I've only just come.'

'I want to write a letter to my grand… to my mother. We'll certainly meet up tomorrow. Don't forget.'

I waved goodbye to the boys laughing behind our bench as well. With a few hand gestures I directed their attention to the fact that the elderly but still good-looking man sunning himself before them was a potential client, at least in theory.

# 16

*Dear Grandma,*

*I spent last weekend mainly lying on my back and counting my vocabulary. 2,310 words it came to, a round number. I readily admit that this is a poor total and so makes it easier for me to exercise moderation and stylish self-denial regarding writing, but I'd be grateful if you would allow me to memorize at least one new word or archaism or phrase every day.*

*Don't worry, I'm not writing stories. I think only on Fridays. Recently I have become interested in sheep and I have noted down two interesting things about them: e.g. that the fury of a sheep is terrible and this set me thinking (only on Fridays!). A completely atypical sheep character began taking shape in my mind. The other is more conventional, yet still exciting: the case of the old sheep and*

*the butcher. The suggestion brings you, too, out in a cold*
*sweat, doesn't it?*
    *For my birthday I would ask to be allowed to write a*
*sheep story. I will not act arbitrarily without your approval.*
             *With tender love: your granddaughter J.*

It would, of course, be over-hasty to pass judgement on the passage of my days on the basis of this letter, for if it was in my interests I was prepared to lie like a rug. At bottom Grandma pinned her hopes on two things: 1. that prohibition suppresses the spirit (see: Bolshevism, Fascism) and 2. that the spies she had put in place to keep an eye on me would see through me. As for the latter: how crass! Even I was not clear about my intentions! It seemed, nonetheless, that Uncle Oscar was not being loyal. He did not put himself out too much for the daily meatless food, and he tended to support the free soaring of my spirit. As for the first point: if it's forbidden, the world of animals attracts me even more. Sentences of the following type cropped up in my head: *this is an ecogarden, the rules of play are different. There is no crop-spraying, you can eat anything you wish. But beware of the stinkweed!* Alas, I didn't have time to preserve them on paper.

My daily timetable constrained me as follows: I got up at 8 and devoted myself to the arts until 11. Since I've had to provide receipts for what I consume, I have perceived it in quite a different light. I did not like to go to exhibitions and galleries because they were relatively inexpensive and time-consuming. I ignored free shows and displays. If I heard that there was a free Bach concert – motets and madrigals – in a church for all and sundry, or distinguished writers reading from their works, entry free, I would just spit. What, then, did I find tempting? Well: theater tickets for the front row! A dance performance, today only! A concert at the Academy of Music! Magazines printed on snow-white paper! Hardback technical books!

I bought tickets but immediately crumpled them up. The expensive books I hid in a corner of the room, putting the receipts in a safe place, then I set off for work. I kept myself busy for eight hours, trotted home, recharged my batteries, then *da capo al fine*. I squeezed the three hours of Hungarian class a week and other time-consuming activities into this routine. This is how I spent my life on the margins of society and reality.

# 17

THOUGH UNCLE OSCAR should have kept me firmly in his sights, for the most part he suggested we meet informally. We kept each other's company like a colony of the homeless from the capital's sixth district. It is sweet and soothing to be an outsider, so we never spoke of 'us', only of 'them' and 'those people'. On the second free day of the long weekend we took a trip into the Buda hills and tired each other out with the bees in our respective bonnets.

'I think ants are Lutheran,' Uncle Oscar declared, crushing an anthill with his fine kid-leather shoes. 'I am, by the way, committed to religious tolerance, but this just now felt very good,' and he knelt down to dust off his footwear.

'What is your opinion of crickets?'

'I don't like that story.'

'From my grand... I mean my mother's lips it sounded especially credible.'

'She is a woman of utilitarian views. She isn't especially sensitive in a social sense, and I wouldn't call her kind, either. On the other hand, she is...' With a furrowed brow Uncle Oscar tried to find a positive epithet with which to describe Grandma.

'Beautiful?' I offered trying to be helpful.

'Yes, her outward appearance is very pleasing. That's indisputable. And she dresses with impeccable taste. It is my considered opinion, however...' He squatted down to admire a marsh marigold. '...that you don't in the least resemble her. You look more like your father, don't you?'

'How would I know?' When this topic came up I always became peevish. Why do others assume that I know the answer to every delicate question, like some talkative gynaecologist?

'Who the hell knows? Some ten or so years ago, when your mother lent me money at an extortionate rate of interest, we became good friends and at that time she told me some story about the very image of the statue of David making her pregnant. But if that is the case, you don't resemble your father either.'

'Genetics is complicated,' I said drawing a line under the discussion, though I was tempted to reveal the secret of my life.

It would be so much more convenient if I could at last reveal that the *ewig weibliche* directing my life was my grandmother. Almost certainly the one thing that even Uncle Oscar knew about vampires was that they slurp down sperm, blood, milk and lick a lot of salty sweat, and if it happened to come out that I was one of these hideous creatures he would be repelled by my company, be he ever so educated and enlightened. I have to live a lie! I shall be lonely unto the grave!

'Uncle Oscar, do you think there is life after death?'

'How should I know? That is the bourn from which no traveler has ever returned,' he said, blinking, with a sweet smile. Still, the perfunctory reply made me angry and I picked up a rock from the ground and motioned in a threatening way.

'What kind of attitude is this, Jerne? Do you throw rocks around every time someone says something that you don't like? Even if you smash my head in, I will still maintain that the question you have posed is imprecise, too general.'

This response encapsulated Uncle Oscar's charm and I let go of the rock. I suggested we go as far as the observation tower, because I had proposed a trip there the following day to O. and I wanted to check out the lie of the land.

# 18

ALL MY EFFORTS and preparations were in vain. O. just about managed to drag herself out from the shadow of the doorway in dark glasses and urban attire, when bright and early the following morning I called up to the sixth floor saying 'your tour guide has arrived.'

'I'm not going anywhere today. Let's have some tea and a stroll along the promenade. The nightlife that I prefer has taken its toll on the resources that I have reserved for athletic activities,' she said and as she pushed forward her sunglasses a flash of the bags under her eyes was revealed. The poor little girl. It was a good thing that it was not the day they were to take a picture of her for the inside flap of her debut volume. I felt particularly close to her that day, for all night I had elaborated in my dreams on the next steps in our passionate affair. Recently I had felt almost sorry that she did not fall upon my neck as soon as she saw me, since in our nightlife I had just about prepared myself for this and other stomach-churning intimacies.

Half an hour later we were strolling around a spacious square, circling a sizeable band playing prom music. O. suggested we sit down near the band on the terrace of a café with Mediterranean aspirations. They were playing Mozart's 'Symphony No. 40' and I was anxious that the sentimental sound of the violin might gain a hold over me. It's in a minor key yet it's cheerful – isn't that charming? I wanted to share this thought with O. but the relative complexity of the communication held me back.

'Nice music,' I compromised with myself.

'It is. That reminds me: what an adventure I had last night.'

'But isn't it too light, on the sweet side?'

'Possibly, but imagine, last night…'

'What happened?' I asked curtly, to fulfil my interlocutor's duty. I could see that she was going to carry out her intention with respect to the previous night, while I had no such compunction about Mozart.

'I was going to meet up with my friends in a Pest bar. I was on my way there when a young man addressed me in English, asking where he could get a beer nearby. I said he should come with me, I was just on my way to such a venue. He searched my face under the red light and then said he would gladly follow me anywhere.'

I held back a couple of unnecessarily malevolent comments. 'And?' I asked instead.

'When we got there I lost sight of him for a while, but then he turned up again and spent the rest of the evening with me. I threatened him playfully: "Be careful, I disappear at midnight".'

'To which he said?'

'"I won't be surprised because you are like a vision." Clearly he wanted something from me and I was pleasantly, enthusiastically reluctant. I even went out to powder my nose, to get him more excited. And what do I see on my return? He had fallen asleep on the bar and couldn't be roused for love or money. I didn't even get a chance to disappear like Cinderella. I just had to trudge home! Imagine!'

'Hmm.'

I felt that I could safely insert some nice turn into the fabric of the text.

'How could anyone fall asleep in your presence? Such a vibrant, all-female woman.' I was making such an effort that by accident I supplied two adjectives. O. smiled decently, head bowed. I threw in a Grandma-style quotation as well:

'The way you look. Mm! That's something that cannot be read.'

Neither of us was bothered by the fact that O.'s glance was shielded by UV glasses. Though she received my efforts with a relatively benign air, she continued to be as tired of life as was Marie Bashkirtseff before her diagnosis of consumption. In the remaining time we had together I steered the conversation on to a more concrete path: I asked O. to enlighten me about the stylistic function of the expressions 'speaking Pest-style' and 'honest-to-goodness'. This had the effect of galvanising both of us somewhat, but I have to say that, even so, that was another day on which we did not lose ourselves in the labyrinths of passion.

# 19

AT THE END of the Lenten period, life around us was not exactly upbeat. 'Everyone is stuffing themselves to cerebral-haemorrhage level with Easter ham'. Attila kept on repeating this, either hoping that we would eventually laugh, or because the fact oppressed him greatly. It's true enough that the consumption of this type of meat regularly satisfies Hungarians' spiritual needs on the occasion of the resurrection of the only son of the only God. The cook and the waiter felt uncomfortable, as the cultic Easter item of flesh lay hidden in their lunchboxes. The anniversary of my own resurrection was also in the offing but I'm not celebrating it. For me this is neither zenith nor nadir; I prefer to experience it as a rite of passage.

The restaurant was empty, business was stagnant, yet I sat ready for action on top of the dishwasher and watched nature documentaries on the cook's miniature TV. These were mainly about the extended urogenital tract of the female hyena or sixteenth-century ebony carvings, which were intended to show that the world is beautiful and interesting, a place of inexhaustible curiosities. Of course the curiosities were unable to make me forget the fact that my life was fundamentally pointless. My only slight compensation was that theirs was, too. For much of the time I was sad and listless, but then that was precisely why I was there. From a certain angle, then, my mission could be thought of as a success.

I was just cracking cashew nuts when the cook called over to say Uncle Oscar had arrived, though earlier than was his wont, but I could welcome him, since they could manage without me just now. Uncle Oscar gave me a wave with an arm covered in blonde hair. I had the definite impression that he was in a cheerful mood and would not tell me off for being suicidal, nor ask me to read more contemporary literature.

'You may congratulate me, Jerne,' he said at once. 'From today I am not just a Jew who is big-nosed and Marxist, I am also a rich Jew.'

'If your goal in life was to live up to your stereotype, you can now die on the spot.'

'Don't you get it? Grandmother has snuffed it.'

'Seriously? Unbelievable.'

'For me, too. After so many years… You know, Jerne, I'm the kind of person who sacrifices vodka to the house idol…'

'And that is perhaps what makes you so agreeable, Uncle Oscar.'

'…but I was thinking of making a voodoo doll. I've been dreaming of this moment for years.'

'Don't say such things! And there I was thinking what a well-intentioned person you are.'

'I am, it's just that happiness makes me lose my mind.'

'I'll bring you something to drink, to calm you down.'

'Thanks. I couldn't eat anyway.'

The cook suggested an infusion of equal parts of chamomile, lemon grass and wild marjoram. He said this relaxed the nerves and would exit with the urine. In fact what the concoction itself most resembled was a positive pregnancy test.

'What have you brought me, Jerne?'

'Drink it, it will do you good,' I said disingenuously.

Uncle Oscar took a sip and when he saw that we were the only people in the restaurant, spat the concoction out on to the hyacinth flowering on the window sill. In my story it would be impossible to spit on anything but a hyacinth. Certainly not on a violet, rose or heather.

'Forgive me. I'm not behaving like a gentleman, but when I was three, my mother promised me that if I didn't like something I could spit it out. Let's change the subject. It's time I kept my promise.'

'You're going to lend me *Mein Kampf*?'

'Don't you remember? I'm off to New York now for the funeral and the reading of the will. But I'll be back within a month. And from then on your dishwashing days are over.'

'But I have to wash dishes.'

'You are called to do higher things. Let me not hear any modest set phrases. But above all I would like you to join me on my round-the-world trip. I'm starting in Tallinn.'

'Me?'

'You. At this stage in my life you are the person I want to go around the world with. If you are willing.'

'Must I decide on the spot?'

'No. But I will not accept any argument claiming that what holds you back is your sense of vocation.'

'Forgive me, Uncle Oscar, but however tempting your offer, it is necessary for me to suffer for an unspecified period.'

'As you wish.' Uncle Oscar took a slip of paper from the top left-hand pocket of his Tiepolo-blue linen shirt. He reached for a fountain pen in the back pocket of his steel-grey wool trousers, ironed to a razor-like crease but he didn't find it there, as that too was in his shirt pocket.

I thought this was a fine sequence of actions. I watched with my head tilted slightly to the right as he carefully unscrewed the pen.

'Write your address on this piece of paper! I'll send you a ticket for the flight. I'll be waiting for you on 5th June at Tallinn Airport. If you come, you come, if not, not.'

And we left it at that.

# part v

## 20

'COME, KARLIN, let us hurry now,/ come with me up this hill./ The fog has shrouded the forest/ on this autumn morning so chill,' O.'s voice rang out, not bothered in the least that there was neither mountain nor forest anywhere in sight. As far as I could tell it was a very warm spring afternoon and, of course, my name is not Karlin. For some time now we had only been pretending to have language lessons; we called them conversation classes.

O. no longer looked up suddenly when I used the separable verbal prefix correctly. Just what had brought about her sudden longing to be free was unclear to me. For more than an hour her behaviour had reminded me of her rarely-walked retriever puppy: she looked yearningly out of the window and continually remarked that at times like this the only place worth being was outdoors. That was her way of making me suggest we go for a walk. Once out in the open air she cavorted around wildly and dished up a cocktail of poems from the treasure-house of Hungarian feminine lyric. Then suddenly she disappeared out of my sight and all I could hear was her shouting:

'Oh, how he would have liked this,' she said, standing by a low, unfortunate-looking tree and stripping its branches one by one. 'No question. It's dried up.'

'But there's no need to destroy it completely.'

'We often sat under this tree, one of my lovers and I. If possible I will call him this very day and tell him that the tree of our love has dried up completely. Though we have long known it.'

We sat down on a bench nearby. I was already fretful that O. was about to relieve herself of a bout of honesty.

'There.' I followed O.'s pointing finger. 'We stood there on the hill and talked about Dostoevsky. The March wind tousled our hair. When I brought up the hermit, his legs almost gave way. Blood rushed to my face but I kept my composure.'

We both mused a little. For my part because I found this genuinely exciting. The hermit... Quite something. I was almost jealous that such adventures befell O. I too would like to talk of Dostoevsky but, even more, to be a Dostoevsky hero. How exciting those night-time gatherings sound, garnished with feverish debates! If only someone would listen to me all night as I expounded my world view, particularly with no chance to escape: nothing outside except the pitch-black and bleak Russian night.

'...and then he said: "I have *The Brothers Karamazov* in Russian",' O. went on. 'Though he had not yet read it. But he was planning to.'

'And then what happened?'

'He leaned me against a tree and pulled my skirt up to my neck.'

'Despite the fact that it's no simple matter to have intercourse standing upright and it's also uncomfortable,' I said, citing a noted author.

'I agree. In fact he preferred to put his coat on the ground. We lay down and then he again reached under my skirt.'

'Tell me the very end!' I cut in quickly, because I was really desperately uninterested in such obscenities.

'He said the fuck we shared would be stored among his life's most beautiful experiences.'

'That's recognition of sorts, no?'

'Yet it wasn't good. In my view it wasn't very good,' said O. shaking her head. But she was no longer paying any attention to our conversation, though at first it was she who had been so ardently discussing the desiccated tree, Dostoevsky and the positions. Her mind was on something else, which for a few moments was capable of making her forget the fundamentals of her existence.

'Come on, now! Surely it was exciting. It's just time's distortion of once-beautiful memories.' Too far, too far. I wished I could have bitten off my tongue.

'Your Hungarian is very good.'

'Do you think so? I'm glad if that's what you think.'

'I'll knock your block off if it turns out you speak perfect Hungarian and have just been playing me along, goodness knows why.'

I'd had the feeling all along that my acting had been weak, but it seemed that now I had exhausted O.'s reserves of goodwill. It was time to improvise.

'You don't know why? It's because I love you.'

O. bit her lower lip and leaned against the trunk of the tree.

'But it's true that I'm not Hungarian and my Hungarian is not as good as yours. For after all, you're a poet…'

'But why like this?'

'To be with you as much as possible.'

As the scene developed, I was beginning to believe myself, too. I went over closer to O. and starting with her collarbone I caressed her arm as far as her elbow. She stood rigid and in thought.

'Are you very much in love with me?'

'Very much,' I replied, saying it to suggest both intensity but also the struggles of countless sleepless nights.

'Don't worry, I shan't abuse it,' she said pleasantly and turned on her heels.

I gripped her by the shoulders, turned her towards me, then dumbly kissed her, as if the grandeur of the moment had made me uncertain. Again, I found this kind of bodily contact unpleasant. 'The kiss is joy,' as Grandma used to say, citing the words of a thinker unknown to me. This would be fine as far as it goes, but the quotation continues: 'and procreation is lust, which God has given even to the worm'.

With or without God, I am repelled by every kind of ecstasy. But O. began to behave ecstatically: she glued her fleshy lips firmly to mine, her ambitious, careerist tongue scoured my palate. On the other hand it was undoubtedly pleasing to feel a hot-blooded female (hence not hirsute and rather delicious-smelling) human being so close. I was brought up on formula, my bedding was only wood shavings – which though it insulates well, does not keep you warm – so I said to myself: if this is the only way I'm going get my share of the human touch, well, dammit, let's kiss.

We kept at it for a little longer, then we parted, and set off home in opposite directions.

## 21

*Dear Child,*

*Your letter distressed me. I keep wondering how the indifferent child-material that arrived on my doorstep could have turned into such a degenerate mongrel. Where does the guardian's responsibility begin and where do genetics end? Why should I have to put up with your hair-raising idiocies with good grace?*

Such were the rhetorical questions with which Grandma launched into a meditation on how, despite my dutiful behaviour, I was failing to live up to her expectations. She outlined how she would be glad to see more practical initiatives and less theoretical farting about in the way I conducted my life. She ended by evincing her concern over my fate with threats of a murderous nature and her intention to carry them out without further ado should I persist in sharing with her my thoughts about my imagined animal friends.

I had hardly ever managed to do anything that satisfied her. She was always dissatisfied with my progress at school, and she also considered my physical appearance well below par. I had even squandered such recognition as she had deigned to offer *à propos* of my first attempt at sucking blood. Yet how long even that had been in coming, especially considering that the last time she had expressed any pride in me was when, at the age of two, I recited the little piece beginning, 'I'm so little, I'm going to stand on a chair…' at the kindergarten Christmas party.

So long as I'm evil – and we have made it clear countless times that I am – why should my closest relatives happen to be spared evil's rampant offshoots? A fantastic, devilish grin spread across my face as I typed up what I thought of the imaginary little monsters (I condemned them) and my concern that pets of the traditional kind had disappeared from the stories. As a postscript I appended the following:

> *Urgent! What am I to do if there is a dirty high-water mark around the bathtub and I have nothing clean to wear? If the rubbish chute is overflowing and there are disgusting gobbets of toothpaste fouling the basin? Advice please, without delay, because I find my living environment repugnant and uncomfortable!*

## 22

THE FOLLOWING MORNING I was helping the cook lug the carrier bags from the market. On the way back to the restaurant we discussed what dish would be best for using up, at long last, the vast amount of cabbage that had accumulated in the storeroom. I repeatedly suggested that it should be pickled, but the cook's response to this every time was a melodramatic 'But what *in*, for crying out loud?' From the outset he had given the impression of being someone who liked to wallow in a problem before getting round to dealing with it. In vain did I smartly riposte 'In wooden barrels', he turned a deaf ear to this and kept on repeating 'What in?' I snarled finally, 'You have to buy a lousy wooden barrel', but he did not take offense because we were just passing a deli.

We recoiled in horror at the sight that confronted us and watched for several minutes turned to stone, as if under a spell. The neck of a rotisserie chicken impaled on a spit had got stuck in one of the supporting forks and this was preventing the repeated attempts of the apparatus from turning. *Thunk, thunk, thunk.* The fowl's neck was sizzling on the searing metal, its fat coursing its way down in rivulets.

'Horrific!' said the cook when he finally managed to blurt something out.

'At least it's past caring,' I said, referring to the chicken, and proposed that we inform somebody inside.

The cook shouted me down, saying 'we don't engage in dialog with butchers and slaughterers', but he now remembered we hadn't bought either broccoli or curly parsley, so he put all four baskets on his stronger arm and decided to send me back to the market. As he listed all the things I was not to buy under any circumstances, my legs were still trembling because of what I had seen, which recalled the darkest acts of the Spanish Inquisition. Attila's principles had done their work on me: he regarded the idea of roasting a creature whole as an act of abomination, the desecration of a corpse. As I tiptoed away, I caught sight of O.

'Don't you dare buy anything that's wilting!' the cook added but I was already fixed on O.

She had noticed me too. Since our exchange of kisses the previous day I could think of her only with emotion.

'Hiya,' I said, feverishly scouring my brain for something nice and beautiful to say. 'I could hardly wait to see you again. You're looking good.'

I had an inkling that this was not exactly a triumph of sophistication, but it did the trick. The pink glow that suffused O.'s cheeks was visible even through her make-up.

'Why didn't you call to arrange our next lesson?'

'I didn't dare disturb you,' I said with suppressed passion.

'Don't hesitate to call.'

'Thank you. But you must excuse me just now, duty calls,' and I took a deliberate step or two.

'So, I look forward to your call,' she waved and walked on.

'Who was that slut?' the cook inquired but I was already sprinting towards the market.

I had been sleeping for months with *Les Liaisons Dangereuses* under my pillow but until then I had been relying solely on the book's power as a talisman and not learning the techniques within. Still, as I weighed up the situation I concluded that my confusion with the grilled chicken had been of useful service in this brief little interaction.

# 23

THAT EVENING I got home relatively early. I tried to think of some stylish way of spending the remaining hours of daylight. I wondered what a person living alone would do, if she wanted to spend the evening in a cultivated manner and was too tired to focus on pages filled with letters. I had a jigsaw relief map of Hungary – I'd got this from Grandma just before going to Winterwood, as she didn't want me to forget the country's borders – and it seemed like a good idea, since I could use it to advance my geographical knowledge while simultaneously engaging in a quality pastime.

I took out the pieces and spread them out on the coffin, pulled up a chair, and began to put the first of the brown pieces together. My eyes almost jumped out of their sockets when the coffin lid suddenly moved and Grandma climbed out of it in a leisurely manner.

'You?' I asked after a long, long pause.

'What? Do you want me to slap you across the face?' said Grandma by way of greeting.

'You think that would be justified?' I asked pertly but a tiny teardrop wended its way down my cheek. The tense family atmosphere began to be too much for me. I'm a hypersensitive artist, everything pains me ten times as much. 'Is that what you've come for?'

'No. I've come to keep an eye on you. It's only a two-and-a-half hour flight from Helsinki.'

'How are you?'

'You know, Finland is not a particularly fascinating place. My business affairs mean I have to live out in the country, in a red log cabin, by the edge of the forest. Peace, quiet, pure air, friendly people: there are few things which I hate more. But the money makes up for it.'

'What do you want to spend it on?'

'I don't want to spend it – that would be painful. It's the vast sums of money in themselves that are fantastic. The fact itself. There is a price to pay, of course. Do you know what I do at weekends? I go into the forest and scare people. Pathetic. Hungary!' – Grandma let out a sigh as she glanced at the jigsaw. '... My dear, I'm not exaggerating, but tears welled up in my eyes when I saw the national flag flying at the airport. Red for blood, green for bile; happy is the person that sucks blood here.'

Meanwhile I was trying to pick up the scattered pieces. I was on all fours, crawling about on my knees.

'*Virgo intacta*. You are unreliable.'

'Only as a narrator. I'm working on it. It's all in hand. The deed will be done this week.'

'Listen and lower your eyes! Of course you'll manage to pull it off somehow. Even a blind man may hit the mark. But where's the flair, the individuality, the dynamism? The vampire *Schwung*? How many times have I given you an extension? I was deluding myself. It was all in vain.'

I couldn't find Budapest and its agglomeration on the floor, so I retorted angrily:

'Drop it.'

Grandma looked for somewhere to settle down and did so. She looked me up and down, as I, having given up the hunt for the capital, tried to reduce the chaos in my immediate environment, for there was now disorder both in essence and in form.

'You know, Jerne, for me thinking is the core of my being. And now that I have had time to reflect, I have realized that for the nuclear family to live together when the descendants no longer need to be looked after is simply perverse. On top of that, why should the bonds of being a relative oblige me to be sympathetic and ready to help, if such things do not come naturally from within? Take you, for example. I find you repulsive and brainless.'

'You, on the other hand, are gorgeous and clever.'

'Yes. Because I was not born of a sexual act.' Grandma's eyes chanced to alight on my shrine to Oscar Wilde.

'Change the water the chrysanthemums are in,' she instructed me crisply. 'If they don't get fresh water regularly they rapidly wilt.'

I went off at once and released a powerful stream of water from the bathroom tap. Grandma was lost in her memories:

'He was like a giant slug. I wouldn't have sucked out his blood. Perhaps he didn't have any blood… Snails and slugs don't have any.'

I placed a jarful of fresh water under the picture on the wall, arranged the flowers and, plucking the head off one, stuck it on the picture frame.

'I'll have to be off if I'm to catch the evening flight. I wasn't pleased that we met, but I am concerned with you out of habit. What can I say? Try and do what pleases me and then there will be no trouble,' said Grandma, offering a final precept, and reached for her handbag.

'Bye, Gran,' I said and went back to my jigsaw.

# 24

'I AM GROWING to resemble my sign of the zodiac more and more,' O. squealed in ecstasy. She was leafing through a glossy magazine while I was having to read her poems from the issues of *Up-and-Coming Literature* lying on the table. 'At first I had nothing to do with this sign, but now the description fits me to a T.'

This was an afternoon when I found O. pleasant and kind. Her slight confusion made her forget her welcoming routine and also moderated her chatter. She was showing off her poems, but in good taste. In fact, in her love poetry O. extended the framework of the genre to both the living and the dead. She worked through the experiences of her relationships, or toyed with the idea of what a suitable couple she and Walther von der Vogelweide would make. She deployed numerous images involving empty vessels and various liquids. She had just treated me to a reading of her latest poem on premenstrual tension. We enjoyed it hugely. It is the beginning of a love affair that is especially interesting and beautiful, and now it was a little like that. When I had called her a few days earlier I begged her to let me return in person the textbook I had borrowed. She agreed and summoned me over for 5.00 on Sunday afternoon. Since then, that is, for the past hour, we had been passing the time in a leisurely fashion.

O. was showing off in front of me, cat-like – shoulders pulled up, breasts out, back straight, rear sticking out – and, somewhat girlishly, closed the window on to the inner courtyard. When barefoot, she always walked on tiptoe, to tense her body and thus make it seem more desirable.

'What an unbearable racket!'

To judge by his voice a not too well brought up middle-aged man was rowing outside.

'It's the man on the ground floor. He's shouting at his partner because she's not made him dinner.'

'Best not to joke with his sort.'

'Too right,' O. nodded.

'On the other hand, if it really is time for dinner, I'd better be off…'

'What's the rush? Stay a while longer,' she said in a suggestively scary, hushed voice. My eyes began automatically to search for an emergency exit. O. was heading in my direction threateningly. On her face was the conviction that she was now attractive and irresistible. She was pushing, pushing hard.

'I've things to do...' I blustered uncertainly.

'What sort of things?' O. queried, puncturing the final balloon that I could have used to escape from my dire situation.

'In the end there is nothing more important than this.'

I pulled myself together, stood up, and walked over to the window to close the curtains.

# part VI

## 25

'FUCK your fucking class-ridden cows,' the cook exclaimed, but only after Attila had closed the door behind him. He was convinced that cows only give milk if they're knocked up. He clung to this view tooth and nail and no force of argument could convince him otherwise.

'And he's had a university education.'

'So? University is where God's prize idiots congregate. You think I'm gobsmacked that he's got a degree? At least I know what a cow actually looks like.'

As the parameters outlined by Attila also fitted me with great accuracy, I was afraid he might ask if I'd ever been beyond the city limits. I quickly changed the subject.

'The peas have blocked the sink.'

'Because you're as thick as several short planks. You use the waste disposal unit first. Can't you get that through your skull? In the end it'll turn out that you went to university too.'

He was on edge. Even a word in defense of the intelligentsia would only have poisoned the situation even more, so I silently bent over the soup tureen, in which the angel-hair pasta had got tangled up. I had not yet risen to the summit of my calling, but I knew enough that in such a situation only soaking helps. The cook was right. I was not mentally present; my thoughts were constantly wandering and I couldn't even claim that it was to an elevated plane.

And especially not that day, for I had gone that morning to an electrical store to buy a 60-watt bulb for my reading lamp. All thirty of the TV sets located in the display section of the store showed Somi giving an interview. I abandoned my search for the light bulb and settled down before a home cinema outfit to listen to the companion of my childhood years. The female reporter, who was trying to look fashionably unfashionable, was just delivering a wild non sequitur:

'Were you allowed a say in the final version of the record?'

'Absolutely,' said Somi, who had a seraphic choirboy image of himself floating before his eyes.

I was so taken with the young man's handsomeness, colorful attire and powerful presence that I went up very close to the enormous screen. Well, well! We have lived to see that he's a great star! He had worked hard for it and now he had made it. This success story had such an effect on me that in the end I forgot to buy my bulb. I'm proud that I am able to laugh at my own absent-mindedness.

## 26

WE HAD BEEN eating petits fours for two hours and had been moralising so much that my lips were coming out in sores. Before that, O. had been proudly showing me objects that had great personal value for her, the better for me to get to know her thoughts and feelings, that is to say, herself.

'I have to be in love. Always. For me, it is a piece of equipment for my work,' she said commenting on her charming mementos, among them the photograph of a bohemian artist: long hair, shirt open to the navel, hands in pockets, cigarette hanging out of his mouth. I know a male of this kind is hardly typical but I laughed so much I gave myself hiccups.

'How else could I write poetry? I don't belong to any social or ethnic minority, and I am also mentally well-balanced. On the other hand my parents are relatively well-off, and support me both morally and financially. What else could raise me to the heights and cast me down into the depths, if not love?'

'Mentally well-balanced? I certainly don't want to meet any mentally well-balanced people. They scare me.'

'OK, I was only joking,' O. said with a laugh. 'I was exaggerating because I am a Cancer.'

'Right.' I let it pass, as if I had understood. 'But I hope you won't write any poems about me.'

I was quite sure I would start kicking and screaming if the situation were to deteriorate that far.

'You little squirrel-pie. You are so sweet,' O. said, laughing it off, and tried to embrace me, but I deftly dodged the gesture. This was quite out of the question.

'Let's talk about love!' I exclaimed enthusiastically, overjoyed to have escaped. This was an unexpected change of tack, of course!

'Excellent idea. How about you telling me about your former loves. Who was the great love of your life?'

Should I own up now to Polkadot Annie, just to save my skin? Her guileless charm and naivety had held me spellbound. As for Pippi Longstocking, I have never since come across so gutsy a woman. But it would not cast me in a good light if I brought these up. Until now, I had felt a passionate attraction only for imaginary creatures, who could be guaranteed not to come to life: characters in stories, heroes of novels or protagonists of films more than thirty years old. The improvisations in the story department had developed my capacity for fabulating to a high level. Mrs Green, who had led the seminar on how to tell bedtime stories, would always say: 'Find a point of reference, and from then on no one will stop you'.

'In what sense?' I lobbed the ball back.

'Just choose one.'

'What kind?'

'One that made you very unhappy.'

One needs a point of reference and a topic, but it follows from the point of reference that the topic cannot be anything but unrequited love. My palate had been scratched by the dry oatmeal cookie and to ease the pain I sipped a little cold tea, and then began.

'It all began in the province of Skåne one dark and stormy night. But I wonder if you know where the province of Skåne is?'

'Somewhere in Scandinavia, I imagine.'

'Indeed. More precisely, it is located in the southern part of Sweden. Once I was spending Christmas in a small town in that province. Because I never spend Christmas in a country that has a Roman Catholic majority. Once you get to know me, you will understand why. I was just on way back from the community college library with a copy of *The Wonderful Journey of Nils* in my knapsack, because I have to say that I regarded it as a very powerful and edifying work.'

'You read stories?'

'Only to practise my language skills, of course. My grandmother had enrolled me in Swedish classes in the community college.'

'You know Swedish?'

'I didn't say that. So, I was just a couple of miles away from the log cabin that served as my temporary lodging, when I was caught in a snowstorm. My heart still skips a beat when I see a snow-covered highway, where cars with snow chains are inching their way forward. That's when I met Annie. She was a feminist theology student and was just spending her vacations at home with her parents…' I launched into the tale and surprised myself at how easily I was able to make it up as I went along. 'Ever since then my heart has beat faster at the thought of cars hurtling their way across dark fields of snow, on icy roads. If only I could be there among them now!' I exclaimed, rounding off the story with a rhetorical flourish.

'You wanted to marry her…?' O. was amazed and one could sense that her entire being was genuinely stunned. Mrs Green would have been proud of me. She emphasized above all that in such a wholly improvisatory genre as the bedtime story, it was important to use affective elements that might at first seem nauseating. Naturally we could make adjustments according to the type of audience, but in the ideal situation we have information about people's individual preferences. I also brought interactivity into play and I was convinced that, through the story, I had offered my audience the emotional satisfaction that it expected of me.

I remember after the bedtime stories exam – which consisted of having to improvise a bedtime story by freely associating on a word – Mrs Green confidentially remarked that I scored well above the rest of the field. My breathtaking fabulation on the theme of ginger hair deserved the highest praise. Then she continued: 'Jerne – I could not get her to stop pronouncing it "journey" – we expect you to produce next century's Harry Potter.'

Harry Potter? Come off it! Writing bestsellers is not my idea of a career. Apart from the fact that at present I cannot put pen, and hence any kind of work, to paper, if I could only let my imagination soar, take the measure of things… Of course this is sheer speculation, but I think I can safely say that if ever I were to produce any piece of writing that attracted a vast reading public and copies were to fly off the shelves, well, I would be profoundly ashamed of myself. Because one might as well throw in the towel if so many people could identify with as uniquely spiritual a story writer as I considered myself to be.

27

LEAVING O.'S APARTMENT, I was still trying to digest what she had told me at the very end of our encounter: that last winter she had kissed Santa Claus on the lips, a Santa that was on the game in Andrássy Boulevard. Because, and I quote, 'he had blue eyes that drove me wild and the cheekiest look' as well as the fact that he was handing out Christmas candy. This kind of taboo-breaking unbridled sexuality absolutely terrified me. I would much rather talk, think and read about these things than actually indulge in them. No doubt she would protest if she heard that I found parallels between us but I think, in this respect, I greatly resemble Grandma.

I burst into loud laughter, as I happened to be passing the Academy of Music and Grandma's affair with Franz Liszt came to my mind. The whole misunderstanding arose from the fact that Grandma somewhat resembled Lola Montez, with whom Liszt, then still known primarily as a virtuoso pianist, was conducting a brief and stormy affair. Of course, according to Grandma there was not the slightest similarity between her and the scruffy floozy giving herself out to be Lola Montez. Be that as it may, it was Grandma that the fiery Franz flung atop the piano in the grand salon of the Swiss pension, not the above-mentioned adventuress.

The whole story has the definitely euphemistic working title 'Indecent Proposal' in Grandma's book, though not a word was uttered; merely, in a rather piquant manner, a quiet *mon dieu* issued from Grandma's lips. (I have no information on what physical symptoms were triggered.) Grandma was not seeking assistance, for the next moment she booted the Gypsy-music -loving composer so hard in the pit of the stomach that he groaned with the pain. The physical strength of vampires is truly terrifying.

'I'm starving.' My progress was halted by a grimy little beggar who had positioned himself in front of me. I was so lost in thought that I nearly stepped on him.

'A powerful argument, but it's hardly rational to distribute small sums to particular individuals. My Grandma will make a donation to the Red Cross and you will get a share of that. How do you think they pay for the soup kitchens at Christmas?'

My carefully considered sociopolitical reasoning reduced the child to silence. He moved respectfully out of the way as I turned into a narrow side street. Just as a minute earlier Grandma had reminded me of Franz Liszt, so now Franz Liszt reminded me of Grandma.

Grandma – now that I've reached this point – was, I think, under the illusion that I hadn't noticed she had set one of her great friends on me, the red-eyed Childeater. By virtue of my age I had not been under the aegis of the Childeater for a long time, but he had always been a purulent opportunist and I was sure he had not undertaken this duty out of pure friendship. I really don't understand it: it's been a good twenty years since, if Gran was unable to keep me under control, she would just whistle and the Childeater would be there immediately, as if he had some lifelong obligation to Grandma. Or was it not him, just a mania that was persecuting me? No, I could see that he was following me, as always. His red eyes, true to his name, glowed in the night.

Generally he trailed me home from work, keeping a few steps behind, scurrying from doorway to doorway. He followed me all the way to the door of the apartment. There he waited, shifting from one foot to the other, in case I left again later. Sometimes he would brazenly insinuate himself into a wardrobe or the bathroom – where I had still not replaced the broken light bulb from two weeks earlier – and hide there until the first rays of the rising sun.

A burning pair of red eyes in the dark, a bat listening at the window, rats chewing at my toes, a werewolf rubbing his rough skin against me on the deserted street – however cheap the tricks were, they made me very tense. Then one night I awoke to the sound of groaning: it gave me the jitters but, fortunately, it turned out to be just the female member of the couple next door on the way to her climax. I live in a partitioned apartment: the walls are no more than an inch thick.

The red-eyed Childeater kept steadily behind me, keeping three or four yards away. I don't have anything to hide, but even so I insist on my privacy. Or at least he should look me in the eye so we could discuss the matter. I stopped suddenly, turned 180 degrees, because along with my supernatural abilities my daring had also arrived. The Childeater retreated to a dark doorway and I could only see his glowing eyes.

'Hey!' I shouted at the deserted street. 'I'm not afraid of you! You only eat children and I'm an adult.'

Then I ran off like the bellwether reindeer in Lapland, in case he caught up with me. This is exactly how I imagine the onset of infantilism.

## 28

MY ULTERIOR MOTIVE was to manipulate a chance encounter with my dear friend Somi. The last time I saw him face to face, he was showing off his snow-white torso, pink silk shirt in hand. Now he was resting his elbows on the bar and ordering apricot brandy. I decided to wait this out from some way off, since the band's new venue operated with profit margins that meant prices well in excess of what I could manage even after I'd gone through the pockets of Grandma's winter clothes for small change. Somi spotted me at once. We engaged in a couple of rounds of conversational banalities and then paused.

'I hear you're king of the castle these days,' I said, beginning with this sentence my attempt to break out of the vicious circle.

'The news is true. We're on a roll. And what are you doing?'

'I wash up.'

'Heigh-ho. Is that what all that studying was for? Are you at least happy doing it?'

'Of course. It's a dream come true.'

'You never were the careerist type.'

'You know how it is. Things get steadily worse, you slide further and further…'

Somi listened intently and as I spoke I caught sight of O. In a novel, not even a metropolis of ten million souls would be a barrier to the heroes meeting by chance, but in this case I happened to have invited her here.

'Come on over,' I motioned. 'I'm over here.'

After the exchange of hellos, I introduced O. to the pleasant young man.

'Allow me to introduce you to a childhood friend. He's twenty-four, successful, a destructive spirit, well within the bounds of profitability. A great star. Right?'

'Yes, I'm a great star.'

'O. is a poet. She's had several poems published in *Up-and-Coming Literature*.'

'No kidding!' Somi showed the requisite amazement. 'Now that's really something.'

'Hiya, I'm O.-ie,' said O., as she'd already had a drink or two.

'Hiya. S. J.,' said Somi, because he was no longer sober either.

'Well, now,' O. began brazenly, exploiting my inattention, 'you resemble one of my old flames, quite amazingly closely.'

The recognition was addressed to Somi and, fearing that this would end up in the nostalgic recollection of another unforgettable fuck, I sent O. off to fetch a glass of cherry juice, even though she had only just arrived.

'So, you're with a woman. This is even more humiliating for me,' Somi said in quite a different tone.

'Come off it.'

'Not only that, but I'm better-looking.'

And how right he was! Somi belonged to the all-vanquishing Teutonic race, while O. had twice won the Virginia Woolf lookalike competition at high school.

'You never called.'

'I'm sorry.'

Somi was about to respond but thought better of it, as O. had meanwhile returned. She put the cherry juice down before me and waited for my words of praise. When these were not forthcoming, she turned to Somi.

'You're a childhood friend of Jerne's, aren't you? What was she like when young? Sweet?'

'Not in the least. She looked like a matricide even then. I was the charming one. I was the teachers' pet. I was a blonde and reached under their skirts. They loved it.'

'I believe you,' said O., laughing, very much taken with the idea.

'Later, when I was in elementary school,' Somi continued, the bit between his teeth, 'I would take the girls into the bushes.'

'What did you do with them?'

'Everything. Everything.'

'That can't be. How old were you?'

'Seven or eight. I don't remember exactly. But I already knew everything.'

'But the girls,' O. interjected on a practical point, 'the girls were still underdeveloped.'

I didn't wait to hear Somi's counter-argument and made my excuses. I went out and in front of some café or pub drew some fresh air into my lungs. The reproductive instinct of the human race is moving, but I find it very hard to understand why individual members of it jam themselves into noisy, confined, smoke-filled places in order to find themselves partners for coupling. Oh dear, there's the language of a Martian again!

Two days later it was the end of May and the ticket for the flight to Tallinn had arrived. If at least I were quite certain there was no life after death it would be easy for me to decide one way or the other. I can understand in principle why heaven was invented and therefore I ought to be convinced that it did not exist. But the presence of vampires, and hence myself, makes an ugly dent in the beautiful theory of the primacy of material reality. I didn't dare think further along these lines, in case I came up with more philosophical kitsch. I often find myself moved when my mind does mental circuit-training laps of this kind.

By the time I wandered back the two of them were already deep in entirely meaningless, flirtatious dialog:

'I've so often wanted to become a lesbian…'

'Me too…' Somi smiled suggestively and licked his lower lip.

'You know, women are more beautiful and more gentle, and men have hurt me so often…'

'Women have hurt me many times, too. I'd still like to be a lesbian,' Somi went on wittily.

'That's certainly an interesting coincidence,' I interposed, to attract attention to my presence.

O. jumped up and excused herself, saying she had to go to the ladies. Somi knocked back what was left of his drink then, putting a hand on my shoulder, he initiated another pleasant conversation.

'Well, what's new, Jeri?'

'I'm wondering. I know that there are the living dead, those who exist even after they have died, but where do they go once they have also departed their earthly existence? Can one hope for nirvana? What do you think?' I asked but only to pass the time, as I knew that even if Practical Atheism had been an option instead of Religious Education, it would have been anathema to Somi at school.

'Not just now, OK? Listen, Jerne, I need to know something urgently. It concerns the nature of the relationship between you and the girl.'

'What do you want to know? I can't promise I'll reply.'

'Would you be upset if – should the opportunity present itself – I were to give one to this pleasant creature?'

'Rest assured, Somi, that it would in no way affect our lifelong friendship.'

'You never were the jealous type,' he said, patting me on the shoulder. 'I'm off now and I'll ask for her number.'

'Don't! Not yet. When the time comes, you'll be the first to know.'

'Whatever you say,' said Somi and left at once.

We didn't see any more of him that evening, though O. kept asking after him. *Sic transit gloria mundi*. It's no longer me that Somi wants to screw. The idea, at any rate, is a good one: it has symmetry and I'm crazy about symmetry in every form. As for Somi and O., I respect them, because they are beautiful and talented.

# 29

IN THE MORNING there was a news item on the radio that the police in Munich had detained a young woman who had been screaming in the street: 'I am a vampire and will bite anyone that comes near.' I hurried with some concern to the internet café on the corner because I had not heard anything from Grandma for weeks. To my relief an extremely vulgar message came from her that very day from Helsinki, beginning 'What do you mean, what should you do, you talentless idiot!' Our relationship seemed to have gone toxic. This year we weren't even taking our vacations together in Siberia. This deprived both of us not only of genuine rest and the opportunity to recharge with reindeer blood, but also of bonding programmes like the one the year before last, when we managed to break up the Samoyed mafia that had been aiming to take over the world. I need hardly say how that was an example of mind triumphing over the power of raw meat.

However, now these are only pale memories. They assist spiritual deepening, though I feel that in my present state any kind of spiritual life, even the slightest scruples, are an impediment. I therefore began calmly to prepare for a decent conclusion.

# part VII

## 30

O. WAS TELLING a complicated story involving two of her friends who one Saturday lunchtime tried to get hold of some kosher cholent because the grandmother of one had a sudden yen for it. I found the story tiresome rather than amusing, as it resembled the formulaic story of the little rabbit scurrying hither and yon to get help for the choking little hen. As everything has its limits, I broke in:

'But this is a topic for a short story.'

'Indeed. But not for me. It's for a minor realist, and it doesn't even have women in it.'

'Sell it. Or send it to that *enfant littéraire*, Attila Hazai. He always appreciates a good idea.'

'No, I'd rather make a gift of it to someone. One of my writer friends has a birthday in a few weeks' time and I've already set aside another short story topic for him. I'll write it up on a nice card. He'll be ever so pleased.'

'A charming thought.'

'Don't be so blasé! The sun's shining upon us!'

'The sun shines on everyone. Even Colorado beetles.'

'Well, where should we go to give you a good time?'

'Nowhere.'

'So let her stay and never see/ The beauty of the autumn dawn,/ Nor catch the magic reverie:/ Embrace, entwine, and all is gone,' she intoned as she performed a little round dance.

My patience was really wearing thin with regard to these little turns and the repeated references to the autumn dawn were also getting on my nerves.

'Is it nervous exhaustion?' O. finally asked. 'What's the problem, tell me!'

I am sensitive and very considerate in my relationships, and all that, but now that it was a week since I'd had the woman, I had got quite bored with her.

'You've put on weight recently,' I said and I didn't give it a questioning intonation, in order finally to alienate her. In my dreams we quarrelled in hexameters and I was proud that I had got this far at least in my dreams, because when awake I can't even scan a hexameter. What we fell out over was a mildly erotic animal story I had written about our relationship. It was not the washing of the dirty linen that she took to heart; she was furious that I had written it up 'badly'. I really had no justification for the use of one of the most everyday adjectives of negative import, and the shock of her intimate personal critique affected my speech center with such deadly accuracy that I was able to respond only in the very constrained manner mentioned above.

Raising our voices we laid into – not each other! – she laid into my work, I into her narrow-mindedness. In my waking hours I no longer desired any kind of versified hysteria. I thought to myself I would leave her without a word, man-like, austerely. I'm not quite sure, but I think it was at this time that the cruel line I recently discovered on my face formed round my mouth. I'm not saying it to excuse myself, but I too have to keep to the terms of the international franchise whereby the vampire is merciless, immoral, conservative, arrogant and aggressive.

O., that real, that mortal piece of flesh, I left to her own devices when she popped into an ice cream parlor. 'Almond and chocolate with whipped cream for me,' I called over to her deceitfully and, once I could see that the stimuli within had completely numbed her senses, I sloped off. I took steps that were at least a-foot-and-a-half in length.

I went off to the second-hand bookstore and there, by the shelf with first editions of interwar prose, I began to cry. I shed fat teardrops upon the fine bindings designed by the Korvin brothers. How I abhor doing this. And the salty liquid (or thin snot?) stung my skin as well. I chose a few charming-looking volumes and then paid for them out of the cultural fund, though Grandma had warned me that eligibility was limited to books by living authors, or those that had died aged under twenty in a car crash, from cancer, AIDS or cirrhosis of the liver. I took an anthology of classical lyrics off the Latin and Ancient Greek shelves, to send as a farewell gift to O. That kind of thing is a nice gesture, isn't it? Then at the counter I handed over a high-value banknote.

'Would you have change for this? I want to make a phone call.'

The lady at the counter was less than delighted but in the end grudgingly threw me some coins.

A few steps from the bookstore I found a phone booth. Somi was not in, but I left the following message on his answering machine: 'Hello, Soma. This is Jerne Voltampere. I would like to heartily commend to you the up-and-coming poetess, if you're still interested. Have a nice spring. All the best.' I added O.'s phone number, and a list of her weak and strong points. After the call, I posted the book of love lyrics to O. No one can accuse me of not dealing with her humanely.

# 31

'IT'S A CRUEL WORLD,' said the cook as he pulled on his sports pullover and grabbed the food container stuffed with leftovers for his family. The sentence before his words of farewell concluded our half-hour chat. We had been exchanging thoughts about the fact that, through the positional advantage he enjoyed, the waiter always put aside the best of the leftovers for himself, always behaving duplicitously when asked where the artichokes in oil were.

'Goodnight,' I said.

As soon as the cook left, Attila appeared with several dirty pots lined with the remains of coconut butter.

'Not more than six. Please wash these straight away. Please.'

'I'd like to go home, it's gone 8.30.'

'Easy in the evening, galling in the morning.'

He was determined, but I threw in the sponge.

'I'm done.'

I had been waiting for the last three days for an opportunity to pack it in, but they were too good to me. Now at last the opportunity to be offended shone brightly before me.

'Take it easy,' said Attila and at once put down the cooking pots.

'I'm resigning.'

'Think it over! It's just emotion that's making you say this.'

'My decision is final. Dishwashers don't have to give notice, do they?'

'Let's talk this over calmly in my office,' Attila said due to the critical situation his pores oozing a double dose of Peace & Love. His office, where I had never been before, resembled a miniature art gallery. Attila's artist friends had overwhelmed him with their work. They were bound by ties of plant-eating.

'Please tell me what is the cause of the conflict? You understand what I'm saying?'

'I do.'

'So what's the problem?'

'There's no problem. I just don't want to work here anymore.'

'Don't you like our little team? Wasn't it good to work together here? Each of us an outstandingly creative person! And how effectively you washed up! We were really very happy with your work.'

'I want to leave.'

'All right. I won't force you. But I warn you I will have to call your guardian.'

'She's abroad.'

'I know, but I'll call collect.'

Attila was already looking for the phone number in his notebook.

'And tell her I'm going to write stories as well.'

'Don't you threaten me!' he replied with a wan smile.

I knew that he wasn't happy either, so I wasn't angry with him. His faith in a better tomorrow was a front, the merit of drug barons and dealers. His misguided good intentions sometimes angered me, but I'm not judgemental: he too is a suffering human being, let's rejoice that he's alive. While he was searching away with his head down in his notebook, I positioned myself carefully behind him. At a pitch an octave lower than my normal one, in a hoarse vampire voice which I still don't know how I managed, I produced the following soulless sentence:

'You think I could leave you just like that?'

He looked up in surprise but did not resist.

## 32

TIRED BUT PROUD, I passed by the wailing wall of beggars in the underpass – perhaps for the last time in my life. The way I could make this day memorable would be if, exceptionally, I gave one of them some money and this thought did indeed cross my mind. Oscar Wilde would have given them alms, especially if they had asked him. Andersen would throw them small change without being asked. But as for Lewis Carroll, he would open his purse only to those under ten. Perhaps he would even arrange to take their picture if they came to see him in his apartment unchaperoned.

But I was not going to give them any money, even today, despite the example set by my idols. Today, as on any other day, I was evil and heartless, quite apart from the fact that I'm going to get my fairy-tale inheritance only a hundred years from now, and even then only if I perform the role assigned to me by Grandma. In a hundred years' time I would be casting euros at the folk of the underpass, should they still be there, but just now even that seemed uncertain. I was on the verge, in fact, of doing the opposite of what my grandmother, mother, sister and guardian had instructed. Indeed, I said to myself: 'Be still, my heart!' (Don't beat so.) But an artist (which I still felt myself to be, even though I had not put a single wretched animal story on to paper for six months) must sometimes rebel, as that for her is the very spice of life.

Arriving home I retrieved a letter from the letter box redirected from our previous address. 'This is a joke,' I muttered out loud, as soon as I saw the word POLSKA stamped on the envelope. I tore it open impatiently while still on the stairs. Edward Leszczycki had written to me. Edward, who had not for a moment been any less of an idiot than me.

*My Dearest,*

*I do remember… we were sitting in the lecture on children's literature of the world. The lecturer was speaking in a language that does not require diacritics and the number of consonants that can cluster together in it is also restricted. By contrast our papers were covered in umlauts and acute accents, and in mine even the consonant clusters were expansive. Each of us was writing our own story. We exchanged a knowing smile…*

*And after that… Those few months… But we should have met elsewhere, in another form, You know that well. And so that You will believe how often I think of You, perhaps You will forgive even my long silence if I journey to where You are living. I'd like to see Budapest for its own sake, but with You…*

*I'm arriving in two weeks' time, on the Cracow train. Will You be waiting for me at the station?*

*Yours, for ever,*
*Edward*

'Stuff you. They haven't managed to fill you with a single drop of dramaturgical feeling? You write just at the moment when I'm about to set off on a trip around the world. And especially: with Uncle Oscar? And to cap it all: you're lying again!' I was muttering, but now only to myself. And then it also occurred to me that he was driving me up the wall with those ellipses and capitals. He is incapable of giving up that pseudo-saintly romanticism.

Dammit, Edward Leszczycki, s, z, c, z, y! But this had long ceased to have any significance. I got to the front door: there was blood seeping out from under it. Inside the red liquid stood in enormous pools.

What a crazy day. I felt like doing nothing but going to sleep. I carefully tiptoed through the pools of blood and stretched out on the mattress.

## 33

LET THE BLOOD FLOW! Let it be ankle-deep!

I too wanted this kind of thing, when the waves overwhelmed me, but now that it had come to pass, I nevertheless thought it was going too far. By the flood of blood a charitable hand had put a murderous threat on the refrigerator, under a fridge magnet. Such a welter of letters is too dramatic in the age of the telephone and the internet.

> *Jerne Voltampere!*
> *I have really had it with you, you degenerate bastard, even*
> *if you are a hundred times blood of my blood. You will rot*
> *where I find you on 6th June at 6.00 in the evening.*
> *Many kisses: Your Granny.*
> *P.S. Don't worry, it's only pig's blood.*

What would the landlady say when she found a blood-red liquid saturating the white pointing of the tiles? And realized this is likely to affect the color of the grout forever? How does Grandma find the time to organize such pretentious performance pieces? These were the kinds of question preoccupying me as I swabbed down the floor. I had to make sure the landlady did not inspect the apartment before I left for Tallinn. There she would not be able to trace me. As for Grandma: five gallons of pig's blood, a letter written in blood – I can only deduce that the express postal services have no moral inhibitions if the customer is prepared to pay.

Then two other questions took shape in my mind. To what extent does my depression and confused state of mind cause me special joy? How far does earthly suffering cause me delight?

Even if I were to suppose that these were evidence of my genius, and that after my death both myself and my work would be wreathed in awed wonder, the answer in both cases was in the negative.

Well then! In that case, why force matters? I had a lick of the congealed pig's blood, but didn't like it, and the fact that some kind of decision was lurking within me would not let me rest. I hoped it wasn't so but I wondered if it was not the case that I wanted to enjoy life and, in so far as I was prevented from doing so, I was recklessly marching to my death? I surveyed the kitchen proudly and then poured the dirty water down the toilet bowl.

# 34

WERE I EVER to open an S&M massage salon, which is hardly likely, I would furnish it exclusively with office furniture: dark veneered chairs and tables, desks with acres of furniture sheeting, faux-leather swivel chairs on castors. I'd recruit a few officials who had learned the trade in Communist times – of course, even the younger ones are clever and ambitious – and I'd launch the undertaking with them.

The reputation of Hungarian girls, the *Vengerkas*, at the end of the nineteenth century was richly deserved: they were readily dispatched to Sultans' harems or to high-class East European brothels. Why should not officials retrained as dominatrixes enjoy a similar success? In today's globalising world the genuine national speciality is at a premium. The German or Finn whose back has been lashed by the whip of a Hungarian tax official will never choose any other dominatrix again. A new generation of *Vengerkas* for Western Europe! This is an original suggestion; French farmers will never strike again.

I would not have liked to leave any loose ends behind. I was keen to sort out the misunderstanding with the tax office which arose from the fact that I had been employed simultaneously as dishwasher and cultural receptor. That was why, on one of my last days of existence on earth, I went to see the tax people. The visit would have been an orgiastic pleasure if it were in my nature to derive joy from being dealt with in a humiliating and contemptuous way. As it isn't, I spent it elaborating the notion of the massage salon in my head. It was a shame that Grandma's letter had been couched in such a hostile tone, otherwise I would have put the proposal to her. She possesses the necessary entrepreneurial experience for the development of a business plan, as well as sufficient capital to launch such an undertaking. I made a mental note to inform Grandma of my scheme when she went through the pockets of my dead body.

'Not possible,' came the answer of the decently made-up lady to my every question, and I got bored with the whole business.

I thought I would rather go home and write my will. Last time death had caught me unprepared, and although I had managed eventually to return to my previous circumstances, I wanted everything to go like clockwork this time round. Washed-down corpse, Sunday best, last will and testament, farewell letter. I prepared an A4 carbon, filled a fountain pen and eyed the blank sheet. But by the time I got to this point, I felt it was all superfluous. For one thing such manic preparations resemble the Christian death-cult; for another, I had no idea to whom I should leave my leather-bound copy of *A House of Pomegranates*. I kicked off my shoes, and without undressing threw myself on the mattress, the only piece of furniture I had left. In the afternoon I stuffed a few small things into my holdall, those that I had grown fond of and then, all that was left to do was to hand the keys over to the landlady.

In the morning, though, one more thing occurred to me. I dialled Somi's number. I let it ring at least ten times. Finally, it was O.'s impatient voice that could be heard at the end of the line.

'Hello? Hello? Who is it?'

I slammed down the receiver. Every woman is a whore. Except my mother and grandmother, because for them this term is too mild. I ordered a taxi to the airport.

# part VIII

## 35

WE TOOK ROOMS in the Santa Barbara on the Roosikrantsi, because Uncle Oscar said it was good to be close to Freedom Square. I heartily concurred. Uncle Oscar and I were immensely pleased to see each other and we chronicled our experiences enthusiastically, neither of us paying any attention to the other. I was just telling him the story of how at an exhibition of jewellery I had found a dead-mouse medallion in an artificial amber setting encrusted with tiny rows of pearls, and this artistic creation – *die kleine Prinzessin* – had a magical effect on me, when I noticed that Uncle Oscar had fixed his gaze on the window sill.

'Look, what a sweet little bat. It's got its little feet trapped,' he enthused.

I looked over and in the sly and hideous little creature recognized Grandma, who was trying, by helplessly flapping her wings, to arouse some cheap pity. She must have arrived by ferry from Helsinki half an hour earlier, if I remember the timetable correctly.

'Its little leg is broken. I'll ask the hotel staff where I can get a vet at this time of night. If we let it go like this, it might get eaten by some nasty cat.'

'Nonsense. It can fly even in this condition, it's not its wing that's broken. Why make such a fuss about a piece of carrion. Let's throw it out on to the concrete.'

I was surprised to detect in myself the will to live. If truth be told, I was terrified that the grim reaper had arrived earlier than agreed. I did not want to die immediately, at any price, as I had started to read one of the gems of world literature on the flight and I was only halfway through. I thought if I stayed up all night I could finish it by morning and still have time to look round the medieval center of Tallinn before the hour of my death struck.

'Wait for me here!'

'Uncle Oscar, what kind of man are you? You have no tears when your grandmother dies, yet you're prepared to run around for a crappy bat?'

'You cannot imagine, Jerne, how much I'm enjoying being able to sort out everything with money,' he said and rushed away to get a veterinary surgeon for the bat.

Now that I was alone with the creature, I opened my suitcase and dug out the flag of Russia's Komi Republic which, ever since I had used it to blind a mountain wolf, I had appropriated for self-defense. It was with this instrument that I intended to push the bat off the window sill. The flagpole was the right length, I used the unfurled flag to push the window open, and gave the animal a gentle shove. At this point something unexpected happened. (What did you expect?) Granny began to flap her wings wildly, and shrieked as she attacked my face, then rose vertiginously to the ceiling. There was plenty of room, as we had chosen the Santa Barbara partly for the impressive internal height of its suites. Once she reached the ceiling she went into a dive. Heading for me. Leaving the flag of the Komi Republic behind, I fled like a defeated army.

I awaited Uncle Oscar's return out in the corridor. He had managed, if not to secure a vet, at least a lidded picnic basket in every way suitable for transporting a sick bat. And a list of the addresses of animal hospitals nearby.

'It's flown away, after making a show of strength. It was just having us on. How can you fall for such a vampirical creature?'

'It just didn't want to appear so helpless. It preferred to gather all its strength and…'

'Let's not overdo the spiritual life of bats,' I said and put a hand on Uncle Oscar's left shoulder. Somehow it felt good to touch that always soft and warm body.

'And I could have done my good deed for the day,' he sighed. 'I could have helped a needy animal.'

'Let's draw a line under this now. Aren't you hungry, Uncle Oscar? When did you last have something to eat? On the plane, wasn't it?'

'How right you are. We could go and have something to eat, and to drink… I understand alcohol is very cheap here.'

'I hope that hasn't clouded your judgement? In your financial situation, with your scholarly past…'

'Forgive me. Despite being born into an affluent family and inheriting a sizeable fortune, the difficult years spent in European exile have left a curious imprint on my personality. For example, I picked this hotel because of its reasonable prices. Scary, isn't it? But I will do my best. I will stuff money in people's pockets so they carry out my fancies. See, even this basket I obtained by oiling the waiter's palm. In any case I have an irresistible urge to oil palms. I've come straight from Marrakesh.'

'I'll help you out. Take me somewhere really expensive for dinner!'

# 36

'I WONDER IF *seafilee* has anything to do with the sea?'

'Out of the question. This is a Finno-Ugrian language.'

'But not without considerable Germanic influences.'

'Choose something else. An international dish with a proper noun in it. Look for the following words for example: Kiev, Stroganoff, Waldorf, Nelson.'

'I don't like those very much. It's all very well for you and I to take on the barely concealed hegemony of the Anglo-Saxons masquerading as globalisation, but couldn't we ask for an English-language menu?'

'Certainly not.'

On the way to the restaurant – so neither of us were yet drunk! – we decided that we would not yield an inch and we would not hereafter use English as the lingua franca. If necessary, we would rather grunt. Uncle Oscar could call himself Hungarian by ancestry, I could do so by virtue of my citizenship. Either way, we both considered that a thousand kilometres away from Budapest it felt good to be Hungarian. We had to keep ourselves high on the bastion of Otherness, so we insisted on browsing the Estonian-language menu.

'Then I will risk it,' Uncle Oscar said and turned daringly to the waiter who had arrived on the scene: '*Seafilee.*'

'You know, Jerne, I'm no Orthodox Jew but somehow I dislike pork fillet,' Uncle Oscar said.

'Eat mine. It looks like fish of some kind.'

'And you will have my *seafilee*?'

'I'm not hungry.'

'Come now. Let's eat! Let's revel in the flavors. Eating together is one of the most pleasurable of pastimes,' Uncle Oscar enthused.

As I didn't want to be a wet blanket, for a few moments I closed my eyes to try to summon up from my memory the joys expected from encounters of the culinary kind.

'The Monsignore was a good friend of my father's and when he had to visit the States on some diplomatic mission, he came to see us as well. I, the only child of the family, who was then twelve years old, was taken to meet him. The priest deigned to talk with me even though he had been told that I followed my mother's religion. "What are you interested in, my child?" he inquired kindly. "The role played by the Vatican in World War II," I replied honestly. "The child repeats what he hears," the Monsignore noted to my red-faced father. In my mother's view, my action surpassed a little boy's cheekiness to an unacceptable degree. My punishment was to be locked away in the library that was home to my grandfather's collection of modernist books. For a week I lived on dry bread, water and Hungarian novels.'

We had reached dessert; Uncle Oscar had reached his childhood.

'I came out of there with my mind in a whirl. I never again wanted to hear about pure-hearted naïve little women, who tumble trembling into the arms of *roués*.'

'Well, yes. Two of those are quite enough. Sometimes though good taste recoils even at one.'

'Or do you think I was just too young?'

'I don't think anything.'

'No, my parents never found out. That's not why they disowned me,' said Uncle Oscar launching into reflections on sexual psychology as we finished off our wine. 'I had a difference of political views with my father. It happened one fine summer's day as we were having breakfast on the terrace of our house. There was a scream from next door, because Norman Mailer sometimes began to beat his wife quite early. Apart from this, though, there was silence, everyone was spreading butter on their bread and my father's nose was deep in his newspaper. Then I suddenly gave a sigh and, as if thinking out loud, remarked: "If only I had comrades." Because I felt ideologically very isolated in that family. That's why it slipped out.'

'And?'

'My father slowly folded his paper, rose, and with great deliberation walked into the drawing room. I watched him through the French windows. He took out the phone book, spent some considerable time leafing through it, then made a call. It looked like he gave his card number as well. As I discovered later, he had ordered me a plane ticket to Moscow. All he said was: "Go to your comrades." To this I replied: "Right."'

'And then?'

'And then I actually flew to London. I had the ticket changed.'

'Recently my love life has been a funeral procession. Last time all I could manage was a one-night stand, and that was several months ago. I was really crazy about that man: ever since, I always think of him whenever I see short, balding, overweight men.'

As I too was consuming alcohol at Uncle Oscar's urging, I had the illusion that there was no more exciting topic in the world than my table companion's love life. Leaning forward, with eyes glistening, I noisily drank in Uncle Oscar's words.

'But in due course I calmed down. Sometimes I would read the phone book, rolling names around in my mouth, trying out which sequence of sounds most closely matched the name he had given. I don't actually remember, as I was quite drunk, and it's also possible that he didn't give his real name. Since then, nothing, nothing at all.'

'Yet you are still a very fine-looking man, Uncle Oscar.'

'Others have also said so, but I don't believe it. Do you seriously think so?'

'Absolutely honestly.'

'I'm not fat, am I?'

'You're just in fine fettle, Uncle Oscar.'

'But why don't you just call me Oscar. I know I could be your father, but after our decade-long friendship…'

'If you insist…'

My time had come at last. I did not feel I had to hide my innermost secrets any longer.

'This has emboldened me to ask you something. I don't know what you will say, but I have for a long time wanted… Can I say?'

'Go ahead.'

'You mustn't hesitate to say no if you're not so inclined.'

'Out with it now,' my table companion prompted me impatiently.

'What I have in mind… The thing is… I mean, I wondered if we could discuss Dostoevsky?'

'How long I have waited for you to ask me this!' Uncle Oscar said, his face lighting up.

And that's how we passed the rest of the night.

# 37

WHAT IS OLD in Tallinn is really old – this was my tourist guide's attitude. What was new I could turn my head away from and would look at when it was something that I could see only here. But why should I spare myself, it occurred to me, why should I spare my senses? It is hard to imagine that it's all over, that never again would I see blocks of socialist concrete! This line of thinking encouraged me to take a look even at what was not part of the traditional architecture of this Hanseatic league city.

I preened in my tight-fitting tee shirt, with its logo *Qualis Artifex Pereo*. I had bought it back in Hungary; it was all they had left, as the Che Guevaras had sold out the previous day and the new stock was not yet in. I was delighted to observe how other people eyed my chest in surprise, as this was my last chance to demonstrate that I was both witty and ivory tower! I walked around as if I had not a care in the world other than how I would buy bread and milk. Yet under the surface I was a bag of nerves: I kept glancing at the clock tower and calculating over and over again how many hours of worldly life I had left. Though I knew there was nothing to worry about, so long as I had no urge to be baptized and confess. That would be the sign of ultimate despair.

This nervousness nonetheless took the edge off my ability to enjoy the city, despite Tallinn being a truly atmospheric place, a gem of the Baltic alongside Vilnius and Riga. The Teutonic Knights founded this favourably situated trading city, the gateway to Scandinavia. My guidebook had many interesting things to say about the ancient university town of Tartu, and also about Pärnu – yes indeed, Estonian lacks vowel harmony – but unfortunately I would no longer be able to seek these out. From tomorrow I will be in hell, sinking (but not in Helsinki, haha!). That was a classic example of wordplay, by way of parting.

Oscar spent the day in the art galleries of Tallinn. The only reason I didn't go with him was that I wanted to be alone with my thoughts. Bumptious Initiative came to mind, velvet-jacketed Mole, cantankerous Gopher and the sheep stories, those stillborn attempts of mine. Looking back over my work, I was a veritable dilettante, who revelled in creating things. I respected myself for this. All in all, despite my agitated, sceptical being, in a strange way the Sisyphean work I had carried out in the world of literature was profoundly moving, even for me.

On all this I meditated in the shadow of an onion-domed church. I could see no clock on its tower. Unbidden, it flashed through my mind that Grandma was standing with a rusty trident in the hotel room looking at her watch and cursing away as I hadn't appeared at the appointed time. I started to run: at such a point in life it is not the done thing to be late. A few hundred yards on, I saw a clock tower and eased off, registering that it was only a few minutes after 5.00. I even had time to do Oscar's shopping.

# 38

I GOT BACK to the Santa Barbara at 5.45. To my astonishment Oscar was waiting for me in the doorway, though I had craftily arranged to meet him at 6.00 at the Rüütelkonna Hoone, so he would not be in the way when Grandma stabbed me through my crusted vampire heart. Oscar took me by the elbow and drew me to one side. He spoke in whispers, his face contorted by panic.

'I am repelled by those comedy heroes who lament at length when something quite strange or supernatural happens to them. In the theater or the cinema I turn my head away, if it is on the television I switch to another channel for the duration. In real life I don't want to fall into the hero's trap, but I want you to know: I am profoundly upset even if I'm not shouting and cursing. And now for the facts. When I entered here about forty minutes ago, I was attacked by a black shade. I felt a sharp metal object in the region of my ribs that, following a brief struggle during which I realized the assailant was making a determined attempt on my life, I seized and used to stab the thing.'

'Final outcome?'

'Well, this. A handful of dust.'

'This is all man is,' I sighed, and put down my shopping. The bags were really cutting into my hand.

'Forgive me: it's permitted after cremation but this is not the result of exposure to heat. Hackneyed phrases from the philosophy of religion have no place here just now.'

'You must forgive me, but you have fallen into the category error you mentioned. Accept with grace and good sense matters which you cannot comprehend. Don't complain, don't raise your voice. You say it happened three quarters of an hour ago?'

'Precisely.'

Yet how I had said a hundred times what an interesting and useful alternative it was to study Finnish! Estonian likewise. Less practical, but still a fine hobby. Of course, anyone able to attend to the outside world would have heard, inter alia, that between Helsinki and Tallinn there was an hour's time difference. In one ear, out the other. A true professional, yet forgetting that the devil is in the detail. I'm talking about Grandma, my Grandma, who for this past half hour was past tense.

'Let me see the remains.'

'If you're a materialist, don't take a single step inside.'

'I can't be a materialist because of my ancestry, though it has always exerted a strong attraction.'

I depressed the door handle. Grandma's remains were scattered across the carpet, in the form of dust. Identification was facilitated by the titanium wristwatch that lay glinting on top of the heap. I remember Grandma crowing some months before that she had bought it for twenty-five times my monthly wage.

'You are a knight of the light, Oscar. You have vanquished Evil. Your superb physique truly has me spellbound.'

'Do you think my nerves are bad?'

'Yours are fine, mine are bad. Where can we get a vacuum cleaner?'

'Let the staff clean it up. I'll have a word with them.' Oscar bounded off, waving his American Express card.

'Leave it to me.'

I placed my extended left hand on his chest, to restrain him. I didn't want to have to explain that I wanted to vacuum up my own grandmother myself.

'Zzzzzzzz,' I said to the first woman that I came across as I wandered the hotel corridors. I also gave her a hundred kroon note. The crisis had made me reckless. I put the machine, a small but powerful Western make, under my arm and returned to the room.

Of her remains Grandma would probably have wanted it said that not since Dorian Gray had the world seen such doppelgänger detritus, but if truth be told the whole thing was like a heap of squirrel vomit or cat food. What moved me above all was that from her earthly remains there was missing that grace which otherwise always defined this woman who had seen so much in her life.

I adjusted the vacuum cleaner to a setting that would not scoop up everything in one go, and slowly, reverently, gathered up Grandma's ashes. Even so, the ceremony lasted no more than thirty seconds, and what was going through my head even during that time was how serviceable, on this occasion, would have been a truly poor-quality East European product, with which I could have paid her the respect that was her due. But the influence of the Russians in Estonia had clearly diminished quite considerably. I removed the paper sack from the vacuum cleaner and wrapped it in a nylon bag, which I placed in the outside zipper pocket of my suitcase.

# this is the very end

WHEN I RETURNED to Hungary after my exhausting round-the-world trip, I put the paper sack containing Grandma in a Hungarian wheelie bin. Meanwhile I quietly whistled the hymn of the Székely Hungarians, because that was her song, Attila's son, Prince Csaba, trallalallala… I don't know the words. I know that's how she would have wanted it, since she had spent so many unforgettable years in the Carpathian Basin.

I have managed to recover only a small percentage of the material heritage of Grandma; she took the secrets of countless account numbers with her into the eternal darkness. But what came to light was no mean amount. After we had exhausted every imaginable avenue in disposing of the money, Uncle Oscar and I pooled our resources and set up a foundation so that the assets accumulated by the ancestors could be spent like water.

Now, at last, I have a job worthy of my knowledge and skills. I squirrel away and then dig up my own nuts: as our foundation's curator, I am the one who selects, from among the countless applicants, the most desperately sick adults, the most endangered children, the best-established scholars and the most helpless artists, and then, bearing in mind their race, gender, religion and sexual orientation, I dole out to them large sums of money. I'm doing very well, and thanks to my fortunate nature, it is enough for me to have something bloody only every five or six months.

Though that I do need, very much. If you have money, you'll never want for anything. The other day, though, Oscar did ask whether I still had any literary ambitions.

'No,' I replied, 'I'm much too happy.'

I did not divulge to him that I had, however, written this.

Budapest, June 2001.